THE FORTUNES OF TEXAS

Follow the lives and loves of a complex family with a rich history and deep ties in the Lone Star State

THE WEDDING GIFT

The town of Rambling Rose, Texas, is brimming with excitement over the upcoming wedding of five Fortune couples! They're scheduled to tie the knot on New Year's Eve, but one wedding gift arrives early, setting off a mystery that could send shock waves through the entire Fortune family...

As the youngest of seven siblings, Belle Fortune has never backed down from a challenge, not even one as tough as Jack Radcliffe. The hunky ex-soldier loves dogs and looks great in a tux, but he's emotionally unavailable, while Belle wears her heart on her designer sleeves. He doesn't "do" commitment—so why can't Belle walk away before she gets hurt?

Dear Reader,

I don't know if I'd go so far as to say Jack Radcliffe is a "grumpy" hero, but he's definitely a solemn one. Fresh out of the service and haunted by nightmares, he's determined to find a job and just get through his days with as little drama as possible. When he meets our sunshine heroine, her boundless energy knocks his no-drama plans completely off-track. Jack finds himself daring her to take chances—with him. Belle Fortune is the youngest of seven—she *never* turns down a dare. Not even from the oh-so-serious veteran who rents a house solely because it has a nice yard for the three-legged rescue dog he's adopted.

What an absolute thrill it was to be invited to write my first Fortunes of Texas romance for Harlequin! This continuity series is legendary, and I jumped at the opportunity to join the long list of incredible authors who've built the Fortunes of Texas family tree. I had so much fun writing Jack and Belle's story. Their personalities really shone for me, and I hope you enjoy their romance as much as I did!

The authors from the Fortunes of Texas series could not have been nicer in welcoming me. They reached out right away to offer tips and support. They made me feel as if I'd joined a really awesome writing club! I want to send a special thank you to Michelle Major, Nancy Robards Thompson and Judy Duarte. You made it fun for a first-timer like me to write a story with details that *must* mesh with *other* authors' stories. As always, a huge thank-you to my wonderful agent, Veronica Park of Fuse Literary.

Enjoy!

Jo McNally

A Soldier's Dare

JO McNALLY

HARLEQUIN

SPECIAL
EDITION

Special thanks and acknowledgment are given to Jo McNally for her contribution to The Fortunes of Texas: The Wedding Gift miniseries.

Recycling programs for this product may not exist in your area.

ISBN-13: 978-1-335-40833-4

A Soldier's Dare

Harlequin Enterprises ULC
22 Adelaide St. West, 41st Floor
Toronto, Ontario M5H 4E3, Canada
www.Harlequin.com

Printed in U.S.A.

Jo McNally lives in upstate New York with one hundred pounds of dog and two hundred pounds of husband—her slice of the bed is very small. When she's not writing or reading romance novels (or clinging to the edge of the bed), she can often be found on the back porch sipping wine with friends while listening to great music. If the weather is absolutely perfect, Jo might join her husband on the golf course, where she tends to feel far more competitive than her actual skill level would suggest.

You can follow Jo pretty much anywhere on social media—and she'd love it if you did—but you can start at her website, jomcnallyromance.com.

Books by Jo McNally

Harlequin Special Edition

Gallant Lake Stories

A Man You Can Trust
It Started at Christmas...
Her Homecoming Wish
Changing His Plans

HQN

Rendezvous Falls

Slow Dancing at Sunrise
Stealing Kisses in the Snow
Sweet Nothings by Moonlight
Barefoot on a Starlit Night

Visit the Author Profile page
at Harlequin.com for more titles.

This book is dedicated to the amazing community of my fellow romance authors at Harlequin—always willing to lift others up and cheer each other on, sharing laughter and friendship.

Chapter One

Belle Fortune was annoyed.

No… That wasn't the right word. Irritated? Perturbed?

She whipped her blue BMW convertible into an open parking spot near the entrance of the only decent shopping she'd found since arriving in Texas—The Shoppes at Rambling Rose. She turned off the ignition and stayed in her seat for a minute, giving herself a firm talking-to.

Only a very bad person would be upset, annoyed, perturbed, irritated or *whatever* just because every single person in her family and social circles seemed to be falling in love except her.

And doggone it, she was *not* a bad person. Belle *wanted* the people she cared about to find love and happiness. It was wonderful. For them. Sure, *she* was the one with ten different Pinterest boards filled with wedding gowns, wedding locations, wedding flowers. And yes, she couldn't help wondering once in a while when it might finally be *her* turn, but… She was fine. Totally fine. Completely. Fine.

Belle shook her head at herself. Self-pity was not her style. She got out of the car and shrugged off her melancholy. Hopefully a little change of scenery would help her snap out of it. The Hotel Fortune had been nonstop romance since her arrival in Rambling Rose a month ago. First up had been the lavish five-couple wedding ceremony of her Fortune cousins on New Year's Eve. The hotel had been filled with happy Fortunes—there were a *lot* of them—not to mention lavish displays of beautiful flowers.

It was a relief when the decor was taken down after the weddings. Unfortunately—at least for Belle—the place immediately filled with lush Valentine's Day decor. Vases full of fresh-cut red and white roses began appearing all around the lobby. At breakfast there were heart-shaped waffles, and at night there were pink "Cupid cocktails" at the bar. Belle had always been the starry-eyed romantic of her family, but she'd seen enough hearts and cupids in just one month here in Rambling Rose to last her a lifetime.

She was only a few steps inside The Shoppes at Rambling Rose when she realized her mistake. With Valentine's Day right around the corner, naturally the shopping center was wall-to-wall hearts and flowers, too. This was the opposite of getting a reprieve from romance! Stores were advertising ways to Make Her Day Special and Show Her You Love Her. The local animal clinic, Paws and Claws, was holding an adoption event in the lobby that promised Unconditional Love. *Of course.*

It felt like the entire state of Texas was going out of its way to tell Belle she was alone when everyone else had someone to love. It wasn't fair. Heck, her siblings had often teased her about how she heard wedding bells with any man she dated more than twice. That may have been true in college. And maybe in the first couple of years after that. But the wedding bells always seemed to ring for everyone except her.

She stopped in front of a storefront display of expensive leather bags and colorful silk scarves. She didn't need a new bag or another scarf. Then again, *need* was never really a factor when she shopped. She started to go into the store, but had to wait for an older couple entering before her.

The silver-haired gentleman slid his arm around the woman's waist, and she leaned into him as he whispered something. Belle couldn't help overhear as the woman laughed and looked up at him, her eyes shining with love. And a surprising amount of heat.

"Teddy!" She slapped his shoulder. "Forty years of marriage and you can still make me blush!"

Belle turned away from the shop, suddenly losing interest in leather and silk. It wouldn't be worth sharing the shop with an admittedly adorable couple who had everything she'd ever wanted. She blinked, thinking of her parents back in New Orleans. Miles and Sarah Fortune had shared a great love story through the years, even after raising seven rambunctious children to adulthood. Maybe her case of the blues was because she was homesick.

It wasn't like she hadn't tried to find someone back home in the Big Easy. But she seemed to attract the wrong sort of men. Too many guys were more attracted to the Fortune family money than to her. Or they wanted a job opportunity at her father's investment firm, or to pitch some cockeyed investment scheme to Dad or her brothers. If not, they were one of the clueless ones who saw her as some bubblehead blonde with lots of curves and no brain. And Belle *still* didn't have a date for the upcoming Valentine's Ball.

A woman walked across the tile-floored lobby of The Shoppes in a flowing black skirt and white blouse. She sat at an enormous harp set up near the indoor waterfall. *Oh, no...* The woman began to play a familiar love song, from Belle's favorite vampire movie. *Enough, already!*

Her phone began to chime in her bag. She couldn't help praying it wasn't someone calling with news of wedding plans, then she quickly prayed for forgiveness. She wanted people to be happy, damn it. When she saw the name on the screen—her New Orleans friend Shelly Conley—she smiled and swiped to answer, popping in her earbud so her hands were free for shopping. Shelly was already married, so she was safe to talk to.

"Guurrll..." Belle started. "I am so glad to hear your voice."

"Getting homesick already?"

She stopped to gaze at those leather bags again. They really were nice. "Maybe. I've got a case of the grumpies for some reason."

Shelly laughed. "You? The grumpies? I don't believe it, Suzie Sunshine. What's gotten under your skin?"

Belle told her about all the romance surrounding her at every turn, right down to the harp music in the shopping center. Shelly laughed even louder at that.

"A *harp*? Like the ones cherubs play? Oh, wow. That *is* a bit much. But aren't you the great lover of love songs?"

Belle went into the shop, glancing around to make sure that cute older couple had left. She pointed to the silver-blue bag in the window and asked the clerk to box one up for her. She didn't need it, but her sister Georgia would love it.

"I think that whole five-weddings-at-once thing has ruined me." Belle handed her credit card to the clerk with a smile. "Even a romantic like me can get romance overload."

"That's not what Madame Fauntegeaux said, girlfriend. Don't you remember? She said you were going to find your very own Tall, Dark and Handsome in Texas."

Belle groaned. Visiting that palm reader in New Orleans in December had been a lark. Shelly had arranged one last night of partying with Belle's New Orleans girlfriends before she left the city that had always been her home. The narrow doorway just off Bourbon Street had a sign saying Discover the Future…If You Dare. Belle didn't believe in that nonsense, but she'd had a few drinks and the other women insisted she had to have a reading. Naturally, the old woman predicted Belle would find a handsome lover in her future.

"Hel-lo?" Shelly called out on the phone. "You still with me?"

"Yeah…sorry." Belle stopped in front of the jewelry store. "Some bracelets caught my eye. You know that lady was a scam artist, right?"

"Oh, come on! She knew Michelle was pregnant, and she wasn't even showing yet."

Belle walked into the jewelry store. "Michelle started resting her hand over her stomach the minute she got the news, so that was a pretty safe guess on Madame Fauntegeaux's part."

"Maybe, but keep your eyes open for Tall, Dark and Handsome…just in case."

"Sure. Whatever you say. Hey, I gotta run. Tennis bracelets are calling my name."

"You go for it, Belle. Retail therapy sounds like the perfect cure for the blues."

They ended the call with promises to talk later. Belle followed her friend's suggestion, going on a shopping spree. She could have done that while talking—she was a pro when it came to shopping. But she was afraid she'd let it slip to Shelly that she'd *already* met her tall, dark, handsome man. She wanted to keep that little project to herself for now. It was too soon to let anyone else in on her plan to marry Stefan Mendoza.

She'd first noticed Stefan at her older sister Savannah's wedding, and his good looks had taken her breath away. He'd been coolly polite when they were reintroduced at the New Year's wedding, but she was determined to get to know him much better now that she was living in Rambling Rose. She didn't need any palm reader to know the long and tangled history of the Fortunes and Mendozas. That entanglement often led to wedding bells ringing between members of the two families. In fact, Savannah married Stefan's brother Chaz Mendoza. Surely Belle and Stefan would be just as happy as they were. Stefan was The One for her.

Although the New Orleans Fortunes had kept their distance from the Texas branch of the family, there had been a lot more contact between them in recent years. Several of her brothers and sisters had already relocated to Texas. When Belle's brothers Beau and Draper decided to open a branch of Fortune Investments in Rambling Rose this year, Belle agreed to come along to be their office manager. She hoped the move would open new opportunities for her. Not in finance, God forbid. If she could land a husband like Stefan with this move, along with her dream of owning her own boutique, life would be perfect.

Belle daydreamed of life with Stefan as she continued shopping. He'd support her when she stood up to her family and opened Belle's Boutique. Her siblings were investors and scientists—they had a hard time understanding her desire to go into retail. Stefan would rub her feet at night after she'd worked a long day at her shop. They'd travel together... Maybe buy a beachfront condo in Miami, where his family was from. And she'd support him, too, whatever his dreams might be. She'd heard the Mendoza family had a winery and restaurant in Rambling Rose. Belle liked wine. And food. She could definitely see herself helping him there.

Her hands could barely hold any more shopping bags. It might be time to head back to her suite at the Hotel Fortune. Her brothers rented a house for themselves in town, but she'd declined their invitation to join them. Her Texas goals were all about gently breaking ties with the family business. Tough to do that if she was living with her bosses. They'd initially been surprised at her decision to stay at the hotel, but they'd quickly shrugged it off, probably secretly relieved their baby sister wouldn't be crashing their bachelor pad. Belle thought living at the hotel might give her a better chance of seeing Stefan Mendoza, but it hadn't worked so far.

She headed through the atrium of the shopping center on her way to the exit. The harpist was thankfully taking a break. Some of the bags Belle carried were gifts, and she'd managed to find a few trinkets for herself. A gold bracelet. A pretty blue scarf. When she walked into the Hotel Fortune with all this loot, she was going to look like Julia Roberts in *Pretty Woman*.

She was lost in thoughts of one of her favorite movies when she caught sight of a dark blur rushing toward her. There was shouting from somewhere, and by the time she realized it was a *dog* barreling in her direction and tried to stop, the momentum of her packages kept her body moving forward. Her silver-blue Western boots slipped on the tile floor and with a squeal of horror, she was suddenly sailing through the air, shopping bags flying everywhere around her.

She grimaced as she hit the floor, her breath knocked out of her. A quick inventory told her nothing was broken. But everyone in the place was staring at her. Her face began to burn with embarrassment...and anger.

"Hey, are you okay?"

A man's voice made her look up from where she lay sprawled ungracefully on the tile floor. One of his hands reached down to help her up. His other arm was clutching a wiggling black-and-white pit bull. She accepted his hand and stood, humiliation scorching her. There were bags and boxes everywhere. Several pair of hot pink lace panties had tumbled onto the floor. All around her, people were staring. Some were snickering. Her eyes narrowed as they settled on the man before her.

"You should keep your dog under control." Her voice was sharp. "Shouldn't that thing be on a leash or something?"

"It's not *my* dog. I just didn't want him getting outside."

He pointed over to the animal adoption event she'd seen when she got here. A large sign behind the table identified it as Paws and Claws. A teenage girl ran over, looking horrified.

"Thank you *so* much for catching Sarge! I thought I'd latched his crate, but I guess not. He's got so much energy." She turned to Belle. "And I'm really sorry he tripped you up. Let me get Sarge back where he belongs…"

"Oh, yes, please, everyone make sure the *dog* is taken care of," Belle muttered under her breath.

She bit the inside of her cheek in remorse. Hopefully no one heard that bratty remark.

The girl took Sarge from the man and snapped a leash on his collar. When she led him away, Belle noticed the dog's strange gait. The black pit bull had a white face and white paws. *Three* paws. He was missing a front leg. It certainly hadn't slowed him down any, or affected his happy grin or wagging stub of a tail. The man scratched the dog's ears and told the girl not to worry. That he was glad to have been there to help.

Belle felt even more embarrassed than before. Falling down was *nothing* compared to her snapping so uncharacteristically at a man who'd saved a three-legged dog from getting out into the parking lot before extending a hand to her. Her cheeks felt like they were on fire.

"I am *so* sorry, Mr....?"

"Jack Radcliffe."

That name was familiar for some reason, but she was sure she'd remember if she'd seen this guy before. His brown eyes were kind, but guarded. His voice was low and soft with her and the animal volunteer. He still hadn't actually smiled, though. He was built like a mountain—easily a foot taller than Belle's five foot two, with broad shoulders that looked rock-solid under the olive green Henley. A slight stubble darkened his jaw line.

"Mr. Radcliffe..." She gave him a sincere smile. "I apologize for behaving so rudely. I just..."

"You expected me to catch *you* first instead of the dog?"

So he *had* heard what she'd muttered. Her cheeks must have been fire-engine red at this point. If he wrote her off as a spoiled brat, she couldn't blame him. It shouldn't matter to her one way or the other. She didn't know the guy. Her adrenaline rush from the fall was subsiding, and she needed to gather her things and get back to the hotel. But her mother's etiquette rules were deeply ingrained in Belle.

"I'm embarrassed you heard that, Jack. You're not seeing me at my best today, I'm afraid." She flashed her brightest smile and extended her hand. "I'm Belle Fortune."

Jack's lips twitched when she said her name. Was that supposed to be a smile? He nodded as if thinking, *Of course you are.*

"We're practically related," he said. "My sister married Brady Fortune on New Year's Eve. A brother of yours?"

"Brady's my cousin. Your sister is Harper?" His eyes softened more at the mention of his sister. For all his seriousness, he apparently had a heart buried under that rock-solid chest of his. She tilted her head. "Harper's wonderful. That multiwedding reception was packed, but I don't recall seeing you there." No way she wouldn't have noticed this gorgeous man.

"I arrived in Rambling Rose yesterday. I'm afraid I missed the wedding." He bent to start picking up her shopping bags. She'd forgotten her items were still scattered across the floor. She quickly snatched up her pink panties and stuffed them back into the shopping bag.

"I can't imagine missing one of my siblings' wedding. I—" She looked up, her eyes wide. "I don't know what's wrong with me today. That's none of my business."

His mouth slanted into the closest to a smile she'd seen so far. "Up until very recently, I was *Captain* Jack Radcliffe. I just got out of the Army and…" His mouth slid back into a straight line, his eyes cooling. "I couldn't get here in time."

Wow. She was really stepping in it today. "Once again, I'm so sorry. And thank you for your service."

He grunted in response, looking away to grab one of her new red stilettos and putting it back in the box and into the last of her shopping bags. He handed the bag to her without a word. He had that steady-stare thing down really well. A man who was always composed. The complete opposite of her own impulsive personality. But she was a Fortune, which meant she wasn't easily intimidated. She gazed back at him, raising one eyebrow as she waited for a proper response. It took a moment, but he finally cleared his throat.

"Um…yeah. Thanks. I'm actually here trying to make up for my absence. I don't dare show up at my sister's without a wedding gift, but I have no idea what they need. I mean, I haven't even met Brady yet. I know he has two boys. And they just had a baby girl. Maybe some toys?"

Belle laughed, and his eyes widened. Jack wasn't only handsome, he also seemed to be a genuinely nice guy. "Oh, honey, no. You don't buy baby toys for a wedding gift, although it certainly wouldn't hurt for you to show up with something for the kids." He glanced around the atrium, looking lost. She couldn't walk away and abandon him here. More surprisingly—she didn't want to. She was intrigued by Jack Radcliffe. More than she wanted to admit. "Come on. I know which store Harper likes. She has a great sense of style."

"You… You're going to help me shop?"

"Sure! Lucky for you, shopping is my superpower."

He raised a brow at all the bags she was carrying.

"I never would have guessed."

Was he making a joke? Still no smile, but the relief was visible in his eyes. She grinned, turning to lead the way.

"Oh, ha ha. I'm exactly what you need, and you know it. Follow me."

She led him into a small shop with handblown glass. One day Belle had complimented Harper's unusual necklace with a cobalt glass pendant, and she'd told her about the local artisan here who did such pretty things with glass. Belle pointed to a shallow glass bowl of dark blue shot with streaks of green and gold. The saleswoman boxed it up. Belle looked at Jack and knew he'd probably just hand it to his sister like that, so she directed the woman to gift wrap it. Jack hardly said a word, watching her in bemusement, then handing his credit card to the clerk. He took the shopping bag and walked out with Belle. Next she stopped at a storefront filled with stuffed animals.

"You need those two baseball bears for the boys. And that little pink one for the baby."

"Yes, ma'am." He did as he was told, coming out of the store with a large bag holding the three bears. There was something endearing—maybe even sexy—about a solemn military man carrying bags of children's toys through a shopping center so casually. They were outside before he spoke again. "Belle, thank you for this." He held up the bags. "If my sister forgives me for missing the wedding, it will be thanks to you." He smiled at her. It was a soft, reluctant smile, but *wow*. Jack Radcliffe had one hell of a good smile. He didn't seem to notice that he'd rendered her speechless. "So…uh…thanks again. And hey, have a happy Valentine's Day." He walked away, heading toward a dark red pickup truck.

Belle finally convinced her feet to move, stuffing her bags into the trunk of her convertible before heading out of the parking lot. She should have asked for his number. *Umm...no!* She gave herself a mental shake. She hadn't come to Texas looking for some random good time. She was looking for a *husband*, and that was going to be Stefan Mendoza, not some ex-soldier.

Even if he did have a heart-stopping smile.

Chapter Two

Jack woke up at the Hotel Fortune, still thinking of that very interesting blonde he'd met the day before. First, Belle Fortune snapped his head off because a dog he didn't even own knocked her over, spilling her expensive purchases. She was all riled up that he saved the dog before helping her. Spoiled much?

Then she did a complete reversal, flashing a wide smile that made his heart skip a little. She'd not only apologized—and seemed to mean it— she'd also helped him shop for Harper. He rubbed his hands on his face, staring into the bathroom mirror and grimacing at the stubble. He reached for his razor.

So which was the real Belle? She was a Fortune, which meant she was probably rich, so…spoiled wasn't a stretch. And used to getting her own way. She'd taken over his shopping mission as if she was his commanding officer. Still, she didn't have to do any of that. Just because *his* sister was married to *her* cousin, she could have walked away after her apology and wished him good luck.

Instead, she'd acted like his shopping fairy. With those big blue eyes and that wavy blond hair, she was a looker, all right. As petite as she was, her legs looked like they went on forever in those skintight jeans tucked into tall, ice-blue Western boots with sparkly stitching. Everything about her seemed to sparkle.

You should have gotten her number, you idiot.

With a last name like Fortune, she couldn't be *that* tough to track down. All he had to do was ask his new brother-in-law when he finally met the guy in a few hours. He pulled on his shirt, ignoring the jab of pain in his shoulder. Jack had a feeling that shoulder was going to be able to predict the weather when he got old. He stared into the mirror, thinking of the day his shoulder ended up injured. *Nah.* He was in no position to think about dating anyone right now. Especially dating a pampered little shopaholic princess who sparkled. Hell, even her name sounded like a princess. Belle. Wrong time. Wrong girl.

His sister left him standing on the front steps of her house that afternoon while he knocked repeatedly. He knew damn well she was home. If Harper was still this ticked about him missing the wedding, things were only going to go downhill from here. She could hold a grudge for years. Maybe coming to Rambling Rose had been a bad idea.

The door finally flew open in midknock, but no one was there. He looked down, spotting a small boy peeking out from behind the door. Jack grinned.

"Hi, there. Are you Toby or Tyler?"

The boy straightened. "Tyler!"

"Hi, Tyler. I'm Jack." He started to step inside, but Tyler's head shook back and forth.

"You can't come in."

"Why not?" Surely Harper wouldn't go so far as to ban him from her house. Then again…

The boy swung the door shut in Jack's face, and he could hear him yelling inside. "Mom! It's a stranger! I didn't let him in!"

He could hear adult footsteps now, and the door swung open again. Harper looked harried, but her smile was wide and bright. He couldn't detect any anger or resentment in it. She removed any doubts about his reception when she said his name and grabbed him, pulling him in for a tight hug. He was holding two shopping bags loaded with gifts in one hand, but he wrapped the other arm around her and held her tightly. Then she stepped back and swatted his shoulder. The bad one. He steeled himself not to show that it had hurt.

"Jack Radcliffe, I'm so darn happy to see you and so mad at you at the same time. I can't believe you missed my wedding!" Her eyes flashed with anger, then softened again. "I think *happy* is going to win out, though. You look…" She scanned him from head to toe, and her smile faded a little. "You look tired. And…different. What's wrong?"

"Nothing's wrong, sis." He followed her inside, catching sight of the two little boys watching from behind the sofa. "And of course I'm tired. I just wrapped up an overseas tour and rushed to see my sister and meet her family as fast as I possibly could." He gave her a pointed look at those last words, hoping to sell the story that he'd told her back before Christmas—that he *couldn't* make the wedding.

"Ugh. Stupid Army," she grumbled. "Come on in."

She led him to the kitchen. The house was surprisingly tidy, considering twin boys lived there.

Harper had always been organized, so maybe not such a surprise.

"Nice place, sis. You had me wondering if you were going to let me in or not."

She handed him a cold beer and poured herself a glass of orange juice.

"I was changing the baby. Brady forgot to get mushrooms for the steak kabobs, so I sent him to the store." She shook her head with a wry smile. "The boys are learning about 'stranger danger,' so when I told them it was okay to get the door, they took that to mean *open* the door, but not let you in. Sorry."

"No problem." He looked around. "I was gone a little over a year, and now I come home to find you married, and mom to *three* kids. It's gonna take a while to wrap my head around that, Harper." He took a sip of his beer and gave her a once-over with his eyes. "You look tired, too. But happy."

Her cheeks went pink. "I'm exhausted. Little Miss Christina Maric doesn't like to sleep at night. She'd rather play and coo. And the boys are still adjusting to a new baby in the house, so they're demanding attention." She leaned back in her seat. "And I wouldn't trade one exhausted moment of it for the world. I *am* happy, Jack." She straightened and called out, "Come in here, boys, and meet your uncle Jack." The name had a nice ring to it.

Toby and Tyler came running. He could see what his sister meant when she wrote that they were live wires. Their faces, especially Toby's, were full of mischief, eyes darting everywhere. These little boys clearly didn't miss a trick. But they listened to Harper. She'd always had a way with kids. The five-year-olds shook his hand solemnly, then squealed when he handed them each a bear.

"Wow! Thanks, Uncle Jack!"

"Awesome! Thank you, Uncle Jack!"

And they were gone as fast as they'd arrived. Harper watched them run off with a tenderness in her eyes Jack hadn't seen before. She'd spent her life being a nanny for other families, so he knew she loved kids. But this was different. This was his sister in love.

Brady walked in a few minutes later, and the two men quickly fell into easy conversation. Jack realized he'd seen Brady at the Hotel Fortune where he was the concierge. He hadn't made the connection at the time. Brady gave him a quick tour of the house while Harper started putting the kabobs together. Then they checked on the baby. He still could hardly believe his sister had a baby, and she'd named her after their mom, Christina. They ended up on the back deck, where Brady fired up the grill. The two little boys were running around the yard, kicking a ball but not seeming to have any real goal in mind other than sending it as far as possible, then chasing after it again.

Brady watched them with a soft smile. Harper had explained the whole family situation to Jack in her letters. Toby and Tyler were the sons of Brady's best friends who had died in a terrible accident, and Brady discovered he'd been named the legal guardian. His life had been upended by two traumatized little boys, and Harper had stepped in to help. And somehow, through all that stress, she and Brady had fallen in love, adopted the boys and become a family.

"So what are your plans now that you're out of the military?" Brady joined Jack at the picnic table.

That was a really good question. Jack had no idea what he was going to do.

"Yes, Jack." Harper walked out, carrying the wedding gift he'd brought. It was still wrapped in the fancy paper and ribbon Belle had chosen. She set it in front of Brady. "What *are* your plans? I thought you were going to make the military your career."

His sister was clearly still annoyed with him. For missing the wedding? Probably. One minute she was handing him a beer and asking how he was, and the next she was poking at him about his plans in that sarcastic tone that used to grind on him as a teenager.

Jack gave her a half-hearted shrug, refusing to take the bait. "Plans change. Now I need to find a job. I thought maybe construction somewhere."

Brady's face lit up. "My cousins have a construction company. In fact, they built the hotel. And the health clinic. And a lot of other properties in town. I'd be happy to introduce you to Callum if you're interested."

"Oh, he's interested," Harper answered for him. Then her voice softened again. "I mean... it would be nice if you stayed in Rambling Rose, Jack. And the last I knew, you didn't have some secret stash of money hiding anywhere, so you do need a job. Callum's a great guy and would give you a fair shake." She looked up at their house. "In fact, we have room here if you need to get out of the hotel..."

Jack smiled and shook his head. "Where did you get the idea that I'm broke?" He wasn't exactly wealthy. At least not on a Fortune scale. But he hadn't spent much during his years in the military, other than the new truck when he got out, so he had a small nest egg stashed away. Enough to last him a few months, at least.

Harper's eyes went wide, and—oh, damn— were those *tears*?

"Sis, I didn't mean…I'm just saying that I can afford the hotel until I find a place. Don't worry about me, okay?"

She looked up to the sky, brushing her fingers quickly under her eyes. She took a deep breath before looking back to him. "I'm a little…hormonal, I guess. These tears have been popping up without warning ever since Christina arrived. I'm your big sister, and I worry about you. I worry about everything these days. I can't help it…"

Brady stood and pulled her in for a tight hug. She sniffled and wiped her tears—and her nose— on his shirt. The guy didn't flinch, patting her on the back and whispering something that made her laugh again. Then he spoke loud enough for Jack to hear.

"You never sleep. No wonder your emotions are right under your skin lately. I'm working from home for another month, and I can handle Toby and Tyler. You gotta let me help more."

"Listen to your husband," Jack said. "You just gave birth a few weeks ago. Cut yourself some slack."

One of the boys let out a bloodcurdling war cry and pounced on the other. They tumbled around on the grass, yelling as they wrestled. Brady rolled his eyes and gave a loud, sharp whistle through his teeth. The boys froze, then backed off each

other and went after the ball again. Brady looked
at Harper with an arched brow. "See? Piece of
cake. Stop trying to do it all."

"Good luck with that, man. She's always been
an overachiever."

"Hey!" Harper tossed a crumpled tissue in his
direction. "I don't need both of my men gang-
ing up on me." Her phone made a sound like a
squeeze toy. She pulled it out of her pocket with a
smile. "That's the baby monitor. She's up." Harper
swiped her phone screen and he could hear the
baby fussing.

"Pretty fancy system."

Brady caressed Harper's shoulder as she walked
by, then turned back to Jack. "Everything's an app
these days. But it is handy. Harper and I can sit out
here in the evenings and still watch and listen for
Christina. Otherwise I don't think I'd get Harper
out of the nursery."

Before long Harper rejoined them, introducing Jack to his niece. She was tiny and pink, with
large eyes that seemed to stare right through him
when they were open. Brady grilled the kabobs
and the boys ran over when dinner was ready. It
was a comfortable enough day to eat outside—a
hell of a lot warmer than it would have been back
at the military base in northern New York. The
conversation flowed easily enough, although Jack

spent most of his time listening and watching the dynamics of two rambunctious boys vying for the attention of their parents, while still seeming to be fascinated by their tiny sister.

Brady and Harper opened the wedding gift after dinner, and he could see in her eyes before she said a word that she loved the bowl. She hugged the tiny pink bear before giving it to the baby. Then she fixed her stare on Jack.

"Who helped you?"

He coughed, immediately picturing blond hair and baby blue eyes. "What makes you think I had help? Damn, first you think I'm destitute, now you act like I'm not capable of walking into a store and buying something for my own sister."

"Jack Radcliffe, if you'd shopped by yourself, you would have given me a vacuum cleaner or something. Not a piece of art. And definitely not wrapped like that. So don't lie to me."

Brady stood and started to clear the table. "Sounds like it's time for us to leave, boys. Help me clean up, and then I'll let you watch a cartoon or two, okay?"

Toby and Tyler groaned a little, but it only took one look from Harper to get them on their feet and picking up dishes. Once they were gone, Harper ran her finger around the blue glass bowl. Jack knew she was waiting him out. And he knew his sister would wait all night for an answer if she had to.

"Fine. I ran into one of Brady's cousins at the shopping center." Actually, that three-legged pit bull ran into her. "Belle Fortune. She said she knew your taste, so I decided to trust her."

"You just happened to introduce yourself to one of the prettiest women in Rambling Rose? I see you haven't lost your touch with the ladies."

There'd been a time when he would have laughed along with Harper. He'd definitely been all about chasing girls in high school. They'd never had a lot of money, but he'd worked hard with his friend's family construction business, and the muscles he'd gained there made him some sort of a "bad boy adventure" for the so-called nice girls. It was all a game to him back then. He'd outgrown that sort of game in the service. It felt like too much effort now. And meaningless. If he wanted to be with a woman, he'd just head to some loud bar and find someone looking for the same thing he was—a quick release with no complications.

"Hey…" Harper's voice lowered, and she rested her hand over his on the table. "What's going on? I feel like you keep drifting away. Does it have anything to do with you getting that medal?"

He straightened quickly, pulling his shoulders back and speaking firmly. "Definitely not.

And there's nothing wrong. You might want me to give you some dramatic battle story, but that's not going to happen." Not because he hadn't seen a lifetime's worth of drama on this last tour, but because he had no intention of talking about it. "I'm home. I'm job hunting." He gestured toward himself. "I'm fine."

"Are you really?" Harper didn't move her hand. "You seem…different."

"Sis, I'm good. I'm still adjusting to being a civilian again, but I promise you don't need to worry about me."

She looked into his eyes and it took all his strength not to blink and turn away. She knew him better than anyone. Harper finally nodded and gave his hand a squeeze before releasing it. Her smile had a dose of mischief to it.

"So tell me how you ran into Belle. I've only talked to her a few times, but we bonded immediately. I love her style. She wants to open her own boutique, and I think she'd be great at it." If she was as good a seller as she was a buyer, he imagined she would be. "She's only been in town a month or so. Even Brady hardly knows her. The New Orleans Fortunes have just recently shown an interest in the Texas Fortunes, and even then it was grudgingly. Miles Fortune was determined to make his own way. I think he still has a bit of a chip on his shoulder about us."

"*Us?* You're a Radcliffe."

"Not anymore." She laughed, brushing her long brown hair off her face. "The world of the Fortunes is all-consuming. But in a good way. They've welcomed me with open arms, even though I'm still trying to memorize all the names of Brady's cousins and their spouses and kids." She propped her elbow on the table and rested her chin in her hand. "Like bubbly little Belle from New Orleans. Tell me how you met her."

He finished his second beer of the afternoon and shook his head when she offered another. He grabbed a cola from the cooler instead and started telling Harper how a three-legged pit bull named Sarge had led to their introduction and how, minutes later, she'd taken over his mission, including directing him on what to buy. Harper grinned at that.

"Sounds like Belle—she's tiny but mighty. So when's your first date?"

Jack choked on his soda, sputtering for a minute before being able to speak. "Uh…never? The last thing I need in my life is a bossy little blonde. Besides, I didn't even get her phone number."

Harper laughed. "Have you forgotten I'm a Fortune? I have her number if you want it. I'm surprised you haven't run into her at the hotel."

He frowned. "Why?"

"She's living there. She has one of the big corner suites."

"I'm not in the suite wing. Just a plain old room is fine for me. Another reason I'm not interested."

It was oddly stimulating to think that he and Belle were sleeping at the same hotel every night. Under the same roof. He shuddered. *No way in hell.* He needed a job and a place to live before he even thought about a woman, and that woman wasn't going to be Belle Fortune in her big corner suite. He couldn't deny she was sexy as all get-out. But Belle was definitely not one-night-stand material, especially being related to his brand-new brother-in-law. And half of Rambling Rose from the sound of it. That was Complicated with a capital *C*. Which was the *last* thing Jack needed.

Chapter Three

Belle Fortune knew how to make an entrance.

When she walked into the glittering ballroom at Hotel Fortune for the Valentine's Ball, she was there for one reason. To catch the eye of Stefan Mendoza. If that meant catching the eye of every other man in the place, well… Too bad for them. And their dates. She'd had it with being alone, and tonight was her chance. She raised her chin and strode across the room in her deep red couture gown.

The ballroom looked stunning. The Valentine's Ball was a candlelit celebration of the hotel's one-year anniversary. She'd heard the first few months were tumultuous, but the hotel was flourishing now.

Her strappy five-inch stilettos clicked on the gleaming floor like gunfire. She was more at home in these shoes than in those Western boots she'd bought on a whim. She'd learned early on that when you're five foot two, you'd better know how to wear heels. Her hair was piled high on her head in an arrangement of golden waves meant to look half-done and casual. In reality, the look had taken her an hour to complete, pinning it with crystal clips. A few long tendrils fell over her shoulder as if they'd accidentally tumbled free.

At first glance, the dress was nothing more than a drape of crystal-beaded netting from one shoulder right to the floor, sweeping behind her in a mini train. The single sleeve was comprised of draping folds of the same netting, and her other arm was bare. Below the edgy sheer gown was a skintight strapless minidress in matching red satin. She was properly covered, but the dress gave the illusion of something very naughty that people *shouldn't* look at, but couldn't *help* looking at.

This wasn't her typical style. At large gatherings she preferred to go with a more classic look— a little black dress, a sleek sheath. Not tonight, though. Tonight she wanted to be the one people would be talking about. The thought made her skin tighten a little, but this had to be done. Because nothing else had worked.

She hadn't seen Stefan in weeks, other than seeing his back across the hotel lobby—and that wouldn't do. Her mouth twisted into a smirk. She was beginning to sound like Cruella DeVille. All she had to do was rub her hands together in evil glee. If she could just get a chance to talk with Stefan, he'd see that they were meant to be together. Another successful Fortune/Mendoza marriage.

Brady and Harper Fortune came into the ballroom together. Harper looked stylish as always in a simple black dress with a wide red belt. She wore a large vintage brooch of a sparkling red rose. She probably found both at the secondhand shops she loved to scour for bargains. She turned to say something to the man walking behind them and Belle froze. Was that…Jack Radcliffe?

Sweet Lord of mercy, that man looked good in a tux. His stubble was gone, and she could see the sharp edges of his jawline and his square chin. The former soldier carried himself as if he was a Wall Street mogul who wore a tuxedo weekly. He scanned the room, and his eyes widened in recognition when he spotted her near the bar.

She was used to men giving her the once-over, but there was something about his look that sent goose bumps across her skin. Jack's eyes warmed with admiration, but without the leering edge she got from other guys. He headed her way, his mouth slanting into an almost-smile that made her straighten and smile in return.

As he got closer, he gave her dress another ogle, then shook his head with that reluctant smile of his. "Damn, woman. You clean up good."

She pretended to curtsy in response, feeling a sudden burst of playfulness.

"Why thank you, sir. You don't look so bad yourself."

He tugged at his collar with a grimace. "Harper conned me into agreeing to come to this thing before she mentioned it was black-tie. Been a while since I was in a penguin suit."

"A little different from a military uniform, eh?" He grunted in response. "You wear it well, Jack."

"I think this whole night is payback for me missing her wedding." His expression brightened. "And hey—I owe you. My sister loved that blue thing you told me to buy."

Belle's laughter bubbled up. "You mean the handblown glass bowl?"

"Yeah. That blue thing." She saw the laughter in his eyes as he looked at her. "Can I get you a drink?"

"Sure. A glass of cabernet, please."

He was back in a few minutes, setting her drink

on the small café table at her side. He let out a low whistle.

"Are you sure you're safe in those things?" He gestured toward her feet. "I seem to remember you being a little unsteady in some low-heeled boots the last time we met."

"Puh-leeze." She waved him off. "I can run faster than you in these shoes. They're more in my comfort zone than boots." She took a sip of her wine. "Besides, that wasn't my fault. That dog ran me over, remember?"

"His name is Sarge." Jack's mouth curled into a smile. "He was making a break for it when you got in his way. Determined little guy."

"Determined to trip me, maybe. You remember his name, huh?"

Jack shrugged. "It's not every day you meet a three-legged pit bull. Besides…" He put his hand on his chest. "*Sarge* is a pretty easy name for a captain to remember."

She started to ask why Jack had left the service, but her target—her future husband—Stefan Mendoza came into the ballroom at that moment. She turned away from Jack, blotting her lips with a napkin then brushing a strand of hair from her face. She pulled her shoulders back, lifted her chin and sure enough, Stefan's eyes met hers. She flashed him a wide smile, reminding herself not to look *too* desperate. She couldn't resist waving at him in what she hoped was her best beauty queen parade wave. Not eager. Just genuinely happy to see him.

Stefan was alone and looked almost as delicious in a tux as Jack did. Tall, with dark eyes and an easy grace. He hesitated, then lifted his hand to give her a half-hearted wave in return. She sucked in a breath, keeping her smile firmly in place to hide the sting. She knew when a man wasn't interested, and Stefan definitely had a look that screamed *someone please save me.* A man walked up to him and Belle could have sworn Stefan looked relieved. The two men walked to the bar on the opposite side of the room, Stefan never once looking back at her. Her smile faded.

"He's not worth your time, sweetheart."

Jack's voice was low and firm near her ear. She spun on her heel, once again embarrassed in front of the man. And annoyed.

"I beg your pardon?" She could hear her New Orleans accent loud and clear. It was always strongest when she was angry. "You've been in Rambling Rose for no more than a hot minute, Jack Radcliffe. How do *you* know he's not worth it?"

His brown eyes held her glare without flinching. "Any man who doesn't fall at your feet after seeing you in this getup needs his head examined."

His voice was as cool and composed as if he was saying *the moon comes out at night.* But his words made her heart skip a beat. Something about him made her chest feel suddenly warm, so she tried to laugh it off.

"This *getup*? Are you referring to my designer evening gown and twelve-hundred-dollar shoes? This is not a *getup.* It's a style. A look. A statement. A..." What was she trying to say again? "And besides...not to brag, but plenty of men fall for my looks without caring about *me.* Trust me, none of them are worth my time."

His jaw tightened and released so quickly she wasn't sure she'd seen it. Was that a flash of anger? His voice dropped, turning rough at the edges.

"You're right. Men like that aren't worth your time. So you know this guy you're making eyes at?"

Belle wondered if her cheeks matched her dress, because her face was burning. Why was she talking about this with a near stranger?

"Well...yeah, of course. We've..." She coughed lightly. "We've met. That's Stefan Mendoza."

"Big whoop." Why was Jack so close? "I don't care who he is. Maybe you need to...I don't know...make him a little jealous? People always want what they can't have."

Jack's head dipped so he was looking straight

into her eyes. He was so close… So very close. He smelled as good as he looked. Like spice and pine. His eyes were a mixture of near ebony, medium brown and gold. Flecks of gold…stripes of gold… rays of gold? *Wait.* What was she doing studying his eyes like this? What was he doing inches from her face? She gripped the edge of the table.

"Wh-what are you doing?" she stammered.

"Is he buying it?"

"Is *who* buying *what*?"

Then it all became clear. The reason Jack was so close was…*Stefan Mendoza.* Jack was helping her. She glanced over to the other side of the ball-room, where Stefan was talking with his brother Mark. Mark was another shining example of the Mendoza-Fortune connection, as he'd married Megan Fortune at the big joint ceremony on New Year's. Stefan didn't have his back to her, but he wasn't paying her any attention either. She was surprised to realize she didn't care what Stefan was doing, though. She was more interested in what this mountain of a soldier was up to.

She came here tonight to win Stefan's affection. Or at least a little interest. That's why she'd paid to have the gown shipped and altered and freshly steamed for tonight. He was why she'd done every-thing—Stefan. But right now, all she wanted was for Jack to kiss her. Right here. Right now. *What is happening?* She licked her lips and saw how his eyes darkened at the move. This was crazy. Belle Fortune was a strong, smart woman. Kissing Jack would be neither of those things. She didn't move.

Jack's slanted smile deepened, but there was a hint of brittleness to it as he shook his head.

"Of course. You'd rather put your hopes in some guy who doesn't know you're alive. You're safer that way. I get it. A guy like me scares you."

How *dare* he? "I'm not playing it safe! And he *does* know I'm alive." She raised her chin defiantly. "And you don't scare me one bit."

He did *something* to her, but she couldn't exactly define it. It didn't feel like fear, but it was definitely fear-adjacent. It gave her the same surge of adrenaline. She could feel her pulse beating beneath her skin.

Jack's eyebrow raised ever so slightly. "Prove it."

She swallowed hard. "Wh-what?"

"You said you're not scared. Prove it. I dare you to kiss me right now."

Belle's eyes narrowed. She grew up competing with six older siblings from day one. She had four big brothers. She *never* backed down from a dare.

She didn't waste any more time debating the issue. She pushed onto her toes and kissed Jack Radcliffe.

Oh, my...

This man really knew how to kiss. His fingers traced lazily up her back. His other hand cupped her face. And his lips on hers were...strong but not hard. In control without ever making her feel weak. The tip of his tongue traced the seam of her mouth. She relaxed and those lazy fingers pulled her against him. Someone moaned. Was that him? Or her?

Jack had no clue what he was doing, kissing this woman. Belle had pricked his pride when she'd swooned over that Mendoza guy, so he'd challenged her. *Dared* her. And hell if she didn't even blink at the challenge. Hell if she didn't press her lips against his and kiss him.

The moment her lips hit his, everything went hot and tingly from his scalp to his toes. Jack had kissed plenty of women in his twenty-five years. Most of those kisses were great. Some were not great. But Belle was... Well, this little lady knew how it was done. She met him move for move, melting against his chest and cooing at his touch. When his tongue brushed her lips, she parted them. Yeah, this was a fireworks kind of kiss.

But they were standing in a crowded ballroom. In a hotel owned by her relatives. She was a Fortune. He forced himself to pull his mouth from hers, ignoring everything his body was screaming at him. This was just a game. It got out of hand for a second, but it was a game. She wanted another man.

Her breathing was ragged. Her eyes slightly unfocused. She was still pressed against him, so he stepped back. They didn't need to be putting on a floor show. He glanced around, relieved to see that everyone seemed busy with their own conversations and not the Kiss That Set the Bar for All Other Kisses Forever. Jack cleared his throat, willing his body to stand down.

"That oughta get his attention."

If only that Mendoza dude knew what Jack now knew. That Belle Fortune was the real deal. Sharp, sassy, brave and hotter than a firecracker.

She blinked at his words, looking confused.

"Oh…uh, yeah. Sure. It should." She didn't seem very interested in checking. Jack reached for her glass on the table and handed it to her. In the process, he checked across the ballroom and didn't see Mendoza anywhere. A sip—more like a gulp—of wine seemed to help Belle regroup. She managed a smile. "Told you I wasn't scared."

He couldn't help smiling in return. She was proud of herself. "You did. Why don't we keep up the act a bit longer, just to torture the guy?" She started to protest, and he held up his hand.

"No more kisses. This isn't the place for that any-way." And he wasn't sure he was capable of pre-tending that another kiss with Belle was any sort of game. "If he thinks you're with me, he might be more interested." Or tortured. Tortured would be good. Let the guy be good and sorry for what he'd missed out on.

"He might." She looked out over the ballroom. The lights dimmed a few times, and people started moving toward the dinner tables. She let out a long sigh. "To be honest, it would help me on two fronts. I do truly want to get Stefan's attention." She looked down at the floor and frowned. He had to tip his head to hear her. "And I also don't want to be alone at a Valentine's dance. It's embarrassing."

"No guy back in N'awlins?"

Belle rolled her eyes. "No one worth asking to drive to Rambling Rose. Besides, I'd never be going after Stefan if I had someone else. Want to join my brothers and me at our table?"

"Will Stefan be there?"

She put her hand on her hip. "Seriously? If he was, *I'd* already be there." She started walking, apparently assuming he'd follow. And just like at the shopping plaza, he did. She had a way of mak-ing him do things he probably shouldn't. While he walked, he sent his sister a quick text saying he'd see her after the meal. Her response was fast and direct.

Blowing me off AGAIN?

He groaned. She still hadn't let him off the hook for missing the wedding.

I'm sitting with Belle Fortune and her brothers.

There was a pause as the bubbles floated on his screen.

Hope they didn't see you kissing their baby sister a minute ago.

Oh, crap.

Wasn't what it looked like.

Her response was swift.

Sure. C U after.

A moment later she added:

She's cute. Have fun.

He slid his phone into his pocket as they reached

their table. Four men stood at Belle's arrival. The two women at the table watched him in open curiosity. Belle introduced him to her two brothers, Beau and Draper. They were opening a branch of Fortune Investments here in Rambling Rose, and Belle was their office manager. He also met her cousins, Callum and Kane Fortune, and their respective wives, Becky and Layla.

Callum was the one Brady had mentioned as a possible job source for Jack, but he didn't want to blurt out his need for work in front of Belle's brothers. Especially once Draper fixed him with a hard who-the-hell-are-you look over their salad plates.

"So you're Brady's brother-in-law, huh? I don't remember seeing you at the wedding." He looked between Belle and Jack. "How did you meet my sister?"

"Oh, my God, Draper," Belle groaned. "Relax. Jack wasn't at the wedding because he just now got out of the Army. Where he was a *captain.* He got here as soon as he could." Jack bit back his guilt over that little white lie. He wasn't used to someone leaping to his defense the way she was doing. She took a sip of wine, then looked up at him. "We met at The Shoppes at Rambling Rose a week or so ago when a dog from some adoption drive tried to run me over."

Draper's expression hadn't changed. He was

firmly in the role of protective big brother. "So you just met and all of a sudden you're dating?"

The guy was looking out for his baby sister, and Jack understood that. At the same time, he wasn't going to sit here and be grilled as if he'd ridden a Harley into the ballroom and smelled like he'd spent a week in the desert with no shower. Belle started to answer again, but Jack put his hand on hers to stop her. He was a grown man—a soldier— and didn't need her covering his six.

"Your sister and I are friends," he said firmly, looking straight at Draper to make himself crystal clear. "We arrived here tonight on our own, saw each other and decided to spend what's left of the evening together. I wouldn't call that *dating*, but you can call it whatever you want."

Draper's eyes narrowed on Jack. "Are you just visiting your sister or are you sticking around?"

"Draper..." Belle warned.

Callum cleared his throat and tried to redirect the conversation. "Ah, here comes the main course. I heard the chef has had this beef aging for months now, just for tonight." He winked at Belle. "I know New Orleans is known for its great food, but Texas has got some pretty nice restaurants, too."

His wife nodded in agreement. "Absolutely. How do you like it here so far?"

"It's different from New Orleans, for sure."

Belle looked around the ballroom. "Not in a bad way. It's smaller. Maybe friendlier because of that. I haven't seen much of the surrounding area yet. We're getting ready to open the offices next week, so I've been busy interviewing for our open positions and organizing things."

"And shopping, sis," Draper added as the waiters served dinner. "Don't forget all your shopping." He looked over at Jack. "And speaking of interviewing applicants, what do *you* do, Jack?"

Belle muttered a few curse words under her breath, but Jack was beginning to enjoy this little challenge with her brother. He was glad she had someone watching her back.

"Right now I'm not doing anything but adjusting to civilian life. I was overseas until the end of the year." Or sort of near the end of the year. "I'll find a job, don't you worry."

"What are you qualified for?"

"Are you freakin' serious right now?" Belle blurted out the question, pointing at Draper with her fork. Her accent went deep. "If you don't knock it off, I'm gonna whoop on you so hard after dinner that you'll be cutting the grand opening ribbon sporting two black eyes." Everyone at the table chuckled until they realized she wasn't kidding. "I'm the youngest of seven, and I didn't survive this long without learning a thing or two about fighting, so you know I can do it."

Her brother held up both hands, sitting back in his seat. "Okay, okay. I can't help feeling responsible for you being here in Rambling Rose, and I don't want you getting hurt."

Her voice softened and she lowered the fork back to her dish. "That's sweet, Draper, but I didn't move away from home just to have another overprotective father figure in my life. You don't need to take Dad's place. I'm twenty-six and old enough to make my own mistakes." She glanced at Jack with an apologetic look. "No offense." Then she turned back to Draper. "You trust me to run the office, so trust me to run my life, okay?"

Beau had been silent this whole time. He straightened, as if just realizing his siblings were going at it. "She's right. Leave her alone." He looked at Jack. "We've got accounting jobs open at the office if you're interested." He gave his brother a sly grin. "And *that's* how you protect our sister. We have a no-fraternization rule at work, remember?"

Jack grunted a half laugh, wondering if all of Belle's siblings were such ballbusters. "Nice try, but I'm not a desk jockey. I prefer building things that last rather than moving money around."

Kane leaned in and questioned Jack, "What do you build?"

"Houses, mostly. Remodeling. Carpentry. I worked for a small construction company near Cincinnati from the time I was fourteen. My buddy's dad owned it. Got pretty good at it."

"Well, Callum, along with his two brothers and I, just happen to run a construction company. We're always looking for good workers, but even more so, good leaders. Your military experience would be a plus."

Callum nodded, then fished a business card from inside his jacket, sliding it across to Jack—Fortune Brothers Construction. "I was thinking the same thing. Give me a call next week and we'll see if we can set something up for you. We're doing some residential projects and we could use crew leaders with actual leadership ability."

Jack wasn't crazy about leading anything. That hadn't worked out very well for him overseas. He was more interested in following orders than giving them. But this was an opportunity he couldn't pass up. He took the card.

"Thanks. I'll do that."

The orchestra started playing and as soon as they finished eating, people headed for the bars and dance floor. Belle ran over to hug Draper, planting a kiss on his cheek. He grinned at something she whispered in his ear and nodded. She turned to hug Beau, too, but he was distracted. He had been all through dinner, looking around as if he was expecting someone. Or dreading someone.

Jack followed Beau's gaze and saw a woman standing near the bar. She was stunning, with long dark hair and wide dark eyes. Draper smacked his brother on the back.

"You've been making moon eyes all night, Beau. Just go *talk* to the woman!"

The brothers wandered off, and Jack spotted Stefan Mendoza standing alone near a corner of the room, a drink in his hand. Was the guy avoiding the festivities, or was he looking for someone in particular, too? Belle noticed him as well. She was staring. Jack fought off the flare of anger he felt. If she wanted Mendoza, it was fine with him. He stepped behind her and took her hand in his, leading her to the dance floor.

If anything, her fascination with the other man made tonight easier. There was no risk of getting tangled in anything serious with her when she was after someone else. He pulled her into his arms, spinning her around until she tipped her head back and laughed up at him. Damn, her laughter made him feel good.

Everything about her made him feel good, to be honest. It wasn't all that surprising to hear Belle was the baby of seven. Judging from the number of packages she'd had on her shopping expedition, she was comfortable with her family's wealth. He wasn't sure how rich she was, but she was rich. Seemed like a lot of the Fortunes were.

Judging from the way she'd taken over his shopping decisions that day, she was also used to getting what she wanted. That might get exhausting in the long term. She was a little pistol, though.

They could have some fun. Maybe sneak in another one of those red-hot kisses. Just to make that other guy jealous. Then he and Belle Fortune would walk away from each other with no messy expectations or complications.

Easy-peasy.

Chapter Four

Belle was still trying to wake up when she pulled her hair back into a short ponytail the next morning, thinking about Jack Radcliffe. What a surprise he'd turned out to be. Drop-dead gorgeous in a tux. And a surprisingly good dancer, too. She pulled on an oversize yellow sweater that fell off one shoulder, and tugged on black leggings and a pair of bejeweled leather flats. She'd opted for comfort—she wasn't looking to impress anyone this morning. She just wanted to get to the Sunday brunch at the hotel's restaurant before it closed. She was in need of some hearty food and a bucketload of coffee after all that dancing last night.

She and Jack had spent a couple hours at the gala going from the dance floor to the bar and back again. Fast songs. Slow songs. Jack didn't have that weird self-consciousness some men seemed to have about dancing. As if they were afraid they'd do something wrong or draw too much attention to themselves. And when the songs got bluesy, he moved like… Well, the man had hip action for days.

She tied a colorful scarf around her ponytail, finished her makeup and headed out to the elevators, thoughts of Jack following her. He seemed to be so comfortable with who he was. She wouldn't describe him as *happy* necessarily—hard to do that when he so rarely smiled. But he moved through the world like a guy who was never rattled by anything or anyone. Mr. Go with the Flow. She found that quality oddly comforting.

And he was generous. After all, he'd offered to help her in her quest to get Stefan's attention. She'd noticed her Mendoza target a few times throughout the ball. Never looking right at her and Jack, but never too far away either. Maybe he was glancing away at the last second. She smiled. She'd be willing to bet he didn't look away from that kiss she and Jack shared if he saw it. Her fingers touched her lips inside the elevator. The man seriously knew how to kiss a woman. Even when it was all an act.

She flinched when the elevator chimed, announcing that she'd reached the lobby. She'd been so lost in thoughts of Jack—and of Stefan, of course—that she'd almost forgotten where she was. The doors slid open, and she was delighted to spot Stefan across the lobby, talking to a man she didn't recognize. Stefan's eyes met hers when the doors opened. Had he been waiting for her? Had the act worked last night? She gave him her brightest smile as she stepped out of the elevator with all the confidence she could muster. This was her moment.

She never saw the man rushing toward the front door of the lobby. Not until she stepped out of the elevator directly in his path. He crashed into her, hard enough to send her flying. Damn it, the bruises from her fall at the shopping center had just healed up and here she went again. Right in front of Stefan. Her eyes closed as she braced to hit the floor. Instead, strong hands gripped her upper arms and swung her around until she came to a hard stop…still upright.

"Holy… Are you okay?" She opened her eyes at the familiar male voice. "*Belle?* What the hell are you doing?"

"Jack?" His back was against the wall, and she

was against his chest. He'd spun and used the wall to save them both from going down. He grimaced, rolling his right shoulder as if it hurt. "Uh…*what the hell* right back at you. Try watching where you're going!" She pushed hard against his chest and he winced before releasing her. "Wait…are *you* okay? Did I hurt your shoulder?"

His expression went from angry surprise to his usual neutral, and his voice lowered. "You're not big enough to hurt me, Belle. It's an old injury. And *you're* the one who stepped in front of me out of nowhere. For a second there, I thought we were both gonna hit the deck."

"It wasn't out of nowhere—the elevator is right there, and the fact that the doors opened should have clued you in that someone might be coming out." She couldn't believe she'd almost fallen at his feet again. She lowered her voice to a near whisper. "Stefan was looking straight at me." She looked back toward the lobby, but he was gone. Her shoulders fell. She was sure he'd been watching her, but…

"Seems to me if he saw you get mowed down by a big brute like me, and he gave a damn, then he'd have checked to see if you were okay." Jack gave a little shrug. "I'm just sayin'."

He'd voiced her thoughts exactly, but she didn't want to admit it. Mendozas married Fortunes.

Stefan *had* to be a sure thing. He simply didn't know it yet. She stepped back, arching one eyebrow at Jack.

"And where were *you* running off to so fast that you didn't see me coming?"

To her surprise, he grinned at her. Whew boy, the man had a deadly smile when he let it free. He patted the top of her head, which was a foot below his head, reminding her that she was in ballet flats. Not a great idea around this redwood tree of a man.

"Maybe you're just easy to miss." He reached behind her head and tugged lightly on her ponytail with its bright bow. His expression grew thoughtful. "Actually, that's not true. I mean, you *are* little compared to me, but you're pretty hard to miss. Sorry—I wasn't looking. I'm meeting up with your cousin Callum, about that job he mentioned last night."

She looked him over. He wore faded jeans and a Henley, much like the day they met, and work boots. The lumberjack look was good on him, but for a job interview?

"Are you sure you don't want to wear something more…professional?"

He chuckled and shook his head. "He asked me to meet him on a job site, so chinos and loafers would be out of place."

"Maybe so. Good luck, by the way. I don't know

Callum all that well, but I've heard nothing but good things about him. He and his brothers basically created Rambling Rose with their projects." She looked around. "The town was here, but kind of run-down, or at least that's what it sounds like. They built the hotel, the shopping plaza, the animal clinic, a spa… They've revitalized the whole place. That's what brought us here."

There was a beat of silence, which of course was when her stomach decided to rumble loudly. Jack's smile deepened.

"The brunch is closing up soon. Get in there and eat something. I'll catch you later, unless you catch Stefan first."

"Hey…" She reached for his arm. "That reminds me—there's an open house at our office Wednesday night. It's a VIP cocktail party for other businesspeople in town and their guests. Would you like to be my guest?"

His brows furrowed, then rose. "Ah…is Stefan going to be there?"

"Yes." Her sister Savannah mentioned he was coming with her and Chaz.

"And I take it he's not going as your guest?"

"If he was, would I be asking you?"

"Do I need a tux?"

"Business attire is fine. And in case you haven't

noticed, business attire in Texas is clean jeans and a sport coat."

He paused, as if in deep thought, but she had a feeling it was all a put-on. He gave her that slanted grin of his. "I can manage that. Is there enough food to count as a meal?"

She laughed. "Trust me, no one will leave hungry. I have to be there early to get everything ready, so you can meet me there. Around five?"

"It's a date. Now go get your breakfast. I have a job interview to get to."

"Good luck!" She watched him leave the hotel, feeling a weird sense of anticipation that he'd be her date on Wednesday. It was only because it would help make Stefan jealous. The only problem with that plan was that Stefan hadn't seemed the least bit jealous yet. Or interested, for that matter. But the plan was worth another try. And Jack was easy to be with. Easy on the eyes, too.

She went into the restaurant, unable to ignore her rumbling belly any longer. She heard her name and turned to see Megan Fortune Mendoza waving. Meg was another of Belle's newfound Texas Fortune cousins. And yes—yet another Fortune married to a Mendoza brother. Meg was the director of finance for both of the restaurants run by her and her sisters. The triplets had Roja in the Hotel Fortune, and Provisions, a stand-alone farm-to-table establishment they'd opened first. So Meg and Belle had careers in common as well as family ties. Belle filled her plate on the buffet and joined her cousin.

"Belle, you look adorable! I wish I could pull off a look like that." Meg was shy—a rare quality in a Fortune. But once she got to know someone, she was open, honest…and funny. "You look like a movie star. No wonder Mr. Hot Construction Guy grabbed you in the lobby." Meg winked.

"He's not—" Well, he *was* hot. "He only grabbed me because he almost knocked me over. And I'm wearing a sweater and leggings, same as you."

Meg looked down at her bright pink sweater and navy leggings. "Yeah, but mine looks like I rolled out of bed and pulled it on half-asleep. You on the other hand, look perky and…I don't know… put together."

"It's the scarf." Belle flipped her hand through the silk bow on her ponytail, remembering how Jack had done the same. "It's all about the accessories."

Meg looked at Belle's sparkly flats. "You should be a stylist or a personal shopper or something."

Belle hadn't told many people here about her dream goal, but she trusted Meg not to dismiss it the way her driven family had.

"I'd actually like to open a boutique someday." It felt good to say the words out loud.

Meg reached over to clutch Belle's arm, excitement in her eyes.

"Oh, Belle! You should absolutely do that! You have such a great sense of style, and women would trust you to steer them right. Would it be just clothes?"

She took a bite of her waffle, basking in the glow of Meg's enthusiasm. Maybe her idea wasn't so crazy after all?

"Mostly clothing, but I'd have a section for accessories like hats, bags, jewelry…maybe even shoes. I might add home accessories, too. Pillows, tabletop art, things like that. Belle's Boutique would be a place where a woman could come for a total lifestyle."

"Belle's Boutique? You've named it already? I thought you came here to run the office for Fortune Investments?"

"I told my brothers that role was temporary, but I'm not sure if Beau and Draper heard me." She adored her family, but she had the feeling a clothing boutique was not considered a lofty enough goal for her supercompetitive father and siblings. "My brothers will probably want me to franchise the boutique and take over Fifth Avenue with it. Go big or go home—that's their motto."

Meg nodded. "That seems to be a common Fortune theme. I assume you have a business plan already? And market research?"

"Leave it to a fellow numbers girl to ask that!" Belle laughed. "And yes, I have a business plan. I've reached out to a few potential vendors. And I've done my research. There are upscale stores at The Shoppes at Rambling Rose, but not a complete lifestyle store like I envision. I want customers to walk in and feel like they want to live right there in the shop. They'll want to buy everything they see, because it will make them feel special and beautiful in their own unique way." She wanted it to be an individual experience for every person who walked in.

"Sounds like the only thing missing is the real estate."

"I don't know. Sometimes I feel ready to make the jump, but I'm only twenty-six. *Am* I ready or is it a pipe dream? Everyone tells me numbers are my gift, so maybe…"

"First…" Meg started, counting off points on her fingers. "Successful business owners *need* to be savvy about their accounting, so a gift with numbers is a plus. Second, you've got the best style sense of anyone I know, so you're qualified regardless of your age. Third, you've put all the legwork in already, so clearly this is what you want. *And* what you deserve to have."

Belle stared into her coffee cup for a long moment before smiling softly. "You're a good friend, and an even better cousin. Thank you."

Meg's cheeks went pink at the compliment. "So you're going to do it?"

"Eventually." Meg started to object, but Belle talked over her. "I made a promise to Beau and Draper that I'd give them a year to help them get established. And I promised my dad—the investment firm is his baby as much as his kids are." Belle drained her coffee cup and sat back with a sigh. "And right now, that means going to the office to unpack all the boxes that arrived from New Orleans on Friday. And I need to get the offices ready for the IT guys to hook up all the computers tomorrow. Are you coming to the open house Wednesday?"

Meg nodded. "Mark and I will be there. I won't let you forget that you have a different dream than your brothers, and that it's okay to chase it."

Jack stood and stretched with a groan. He'd spent too much time crouching under this counter without changing positions. His right shoulder was protesting even more than his knees.

"How's it coming?" Stephanie Fortune Donovan asked, setting an armful of folders on the counter. It was midafternoon on Tuesday and the Paws and Claws Animal Clinic was relatively quiet. The only person in the waiting room was an older woman with a plastic pet carrier in her lap. She was cooing and talking to whatever creature was in there.

"I'm almost done," Jack said. "Just have to secure the file drawers under here and drill the access holes for all the wiring. You still want that where you marked it?" He pointed at the three-inch circle sketched on the beige countertop.

"Yes, thanks." She looked around with an approving nod, tucking a stray strand of red hair behind her ear. "It looks great, Jack. I've been begging my brother Callum to reconfigure this reception desk for months now. I'm glad he hired you, or I'd still be waiting."

"Glad to do it. I should be finished by the end of the day."

Stephanie, a veterinary technician, called the client back to an examination room, and he could hear the mewing of an unhappy cat from the carrier. He crawled back under the desk. This job was uncomplicated, other than the awkward position. But it was for the boss's sister, and Jack was determined to make the custom-built desk not only functional, but nicely finished as well. He figured this job was a test.

Stephanie was family, so Callum would expect nothing but the best from Jack. And it would showcase Jack's ability to problem solve, since Stephanie's drawing of what she wanted here had been sketched onto a piece of notepaper and was completely out of scale. Jack helped her come up with a final design that would give her both extra storage and an expanded work surface, while having the area more open for the staff to get in and out easily. All he had left to do after this was hang the accordion-style gate Stephanie wanted across the opening. She explained that sometimes the staff brought animals who needed extra love or attention up to the front desk, and they wanted to keep them secure.

As if on cue, Jack heard the scrambling of toenails on the tile hallway floor, followed by someone yelling.

"Sarge! Get back here! Somebody stop him!"

Jack stepped into the hallway in time to scoop up the black-and-white dog. Just like he had in the shopping plaza. And just like the first time, Sarge's three legs were paddling the air, trying to launch himself.

"Whoa, buddy. You need to stand down, soldier." Sarge stopped immediately, looking up at

Jack with a tongue-lolling grin. Considering he was missing a leg, this was the happiest dog Jack ever met.

A young vet tech came running up, followed by Stephanie. The younger woman looked relieved.

"Thanks so much. I barely turned away from him to grab something, and he was out the kennel door!"

Stephanie scratched the top of Sarge's head. "He's got so much energy and not much chance to burn it off in here. He's looking at you like you're a superhero, Jack."

"Well, this is the second time we've had this conversation about running away." He explained that he was the one who caught Sarge at the adoption event a couple weeks earlier. He frowned. "He hasn't found a home yet? Seems like such a happy guy."

Stephanie sent the other tech to finish up with Mrs. Blakefield and her cat, then gave Jack a sad look. "Poor Sarge has two big strikes against him. Most people don't want to deal with a special needs dog like him, although he barely qualifies for the title. He gets along great on three legs."

Jack chuckled, making a face at Sarge. "It sure doesn't slow him down. What's the other strike?"

"Pit bulls can be difficult to place. People are afraid of them without getting to know the individual animal." She leaned in to give Sarge a kiss on his head, and Jack swore the dog's eyeballs rolled back in his head in ecstasy. "Between you, me and Sarge—I've been bitten by chihuahuas more often than I have by pitties. And Sarge is such a good boy, aren't you, buddy?"

He could feel the dog nearly go limp in his arms. Sarge loved getting all the attention. The thought of him not finding a home poked at Jack.

"What happens if no one adopts him? Will he be…?"

"Put down? Oh, definitely not. Paws and Claws is a no-kill organization. They've already had Sarge for six months, and they'll keep him as long as they have to. We're getting used to having him around, but he needs a home with a big, fenced yard where he can run and play and tire himself out."

She snapped a leash on Sarge's thick leather collar. Jack set him on the floor, but Sarge immediately jumped up, bracing his one front leg against Jack's leg. Stephanie started to laugh.

"Oh, you've definitely made a friend. You wouldn't be in the market for a dog, would you? He's only about eighteen months old, but he's completely housebroken and has been through puppy school so he knows all the basic commands."

"Except *stay*."

She laughed. "Yeah, except that one. He can't help himself."

Jack shook his head. "I'm still living out of a hotel room, so a dog is not an option right now." He reached down to pat Sarge. "And he needs to be with a family, where someone will always be there to pay attention to him."

"Or you could take him with you on jobs."

"I don't know if I'll *have* jobs yet. I'm still probationary with your brother. And I may not stay in Rambling Rose. My life is way too chaotic right now to add a dog to it."

"I think Sarge disagrees." He followed Stephanie's gaze to the black dog sitting at Jack's feet, looking around as if on guard. "When Callum sees the work you did here, your future will be secure with Fortune Brothers Construction. As far as staying goes…" She winked at Jack. "I hear my cousin Belle might be enough enticement for you to hang around."

He groaned. He didn't want people thinking the wrong thing. "We're just friends."

"Uh-huh." She made air quotes with her fingers as she said, "*Just friends* don't dance the way you two did at the Valentine's Ball. Or kiss like you did."

He scrubbed the back of his neck. "I was really hoping people didn't notice that." Their little dare was supposed to be between them. It wasn't intended to be the floor show. But nothing about that kiss went the way it was intended.

Stephanie tugged on the dog's leash. "Belle Fortune has a way of always being noticed. And when she's flirting with the handsome new stranger in town? Trust me, people are going to pay attention." She started to turn away, then paused. "But be careful. The look in her eyes when you were dancing said way more than friendship." She lifted one shoulder and dropped it. "If you're worried about losing the job with Callum, breaking a Fortune's heart would do it."

"Belle and I are on the same page, trust me." He almost blurted out that Belle didn't even want him. She wanted Stefan Mendoza. But that wasn't for him to tell. "I'm no heartbreaker. There's nothing going on with us other than a little fun."

He watched as Stephanie led Sarge away. The dog looked back before they rounded the corner, and Jack could have sworn his expression said *liar*.

Chapter Five

Belle stared at her reflection in the bathroom mirror at Fortune Investments and grimaced. She shouldn't have gotten ready for the cocktail party here. In the dim light, the metallic bronze walls made her skin look sallow.

"Remind me to talk to my cousins about what colors to use in women's rooms," she muttered to herself. She applied one last layer of matte Caribbean Sunset lipstick and spritzed herself with Chanel.

Her brothers had lectured her about looking "professional" tonight. She figured that was a direct result of the couture gown she'd worn to the

Hotel Fortune gala. Looking professional didn't mean she had to throw her signature sense of style out the window. It was a cocktail party after all. She was in a trim black suit. With a thigh-length tuxedo jacket that was the same length as the thigh-high skirt. Though she'd worn the suit before without a top under the jacket, in deference to her brothers' mandate, she'd added an ivory silk camisole trimmed in lace. Her hair was loose, falling past her shoulders in soft waves. She figured that broke up the severity of the suit and her black Louboutin pumps. Well, that and the six-inch-long bright blue cascade earrings she was wearing.

She turned her head to admire the fun of the colorful plastic rings of all sizes, falling like daisy chains and clicking together as she moved. The suit would make her brothers happy—except the hemline, of course—and the earrings made *her* happy. She could hear the hum of voices. People were arriving. Someday, she told herself, she'd be getting ready for her own open house at Belle's Boutique, and she would definitely *not* be wearing a black suit. But maybe she'd wear these earrings. Maybe she'd be *selling* these earrings.

When she stepped out, Beau saw her first and gave a loud wolf whistle. "You look like…wow."

"She looks like she forgot to put her skirt on." Draper winked to let her know he was teasing.

Belle pulled the bottom of the jacket open. "Oh, please—the skirt is right here, under the long jacket. I can't help it if you guys don't understand fashion."

He shook his head. "And those earrings…definitely not anything you borrowed from Mom."

She laughed. Sarah Fortune was a strong woman. She had to be to raise seven children while helping her husband build his successful business. And with all that, she still had time to build a reputation for her own classic sense of style. Their home in the historic Garden District of New Orleans was often included on local Christmas or garden tours, and was known for its exquisite decor. Mom knew how to make a home comfortable to live in while still being true to its history and beautiful to look at.

"Ignore him. We're lucky you're here, sis." Beau kissed her temple.

Draper gave in with a smile. "I'll second that. Couldn't have done this without you."

"Yeah, I know." She smiled, but there were unexpected tears burning in her eyes. Her family could be…intense. Opinionated. Loud. Competitive. And fiercely loving. "Come on, you two." She stepped between her brothers and hooked her arms in theirs. "Let's go celebrate our new business and try to keep people from spilling wine on the keyboards."

The lobby had been set up with food stations and tall café tables, with a bar at each end of the spacious room. Provisions was catering. A quick glance at the first guests to arrive told Belle that this evening was going to look a lot like a Fortune family reunion. The idea was to invite business owners and local leaders for this VIP opening, then hold an informal public event over the weekend when they did the official ribbon-cutting. In Rambling Rose, many of the business owners and influencers were Fortunes. Or Mendozas. Or Fortunes married to Mendozas.

Her sister Savannah walked in with Chaz, and Stefan was with them. She wondered if Stefan would end up working at the Mendoza Winery. Maybe she could serve tasting glasses of their wines at her boutique to tie their two businesses together. Partners in life and work. To her delight, the three Mendozas walked over to her. *Finally!*

Savannah gave her a big hug. "The offices look wonderful! I'm guessing you had a hand in most of this." She turned to Chaz and Stefan. "Our brothers would have been happy serving hot dogs and beer."

Stefan smiled. "That would have made this feel like a baseball game…which isn't a bad thing."

Belle laughed, and mentally cringed at how loud she was. "A baseball game! That's *so* funny!" *Trying too hard, Belle...*

Savannah arched a brow, clearly thinking the same thing. "Uh...yeah. Are you okay, sis?"

"I'm fine! Great!" *Why am I yelling?* She took a quick breath and looked at Stefan. "Would you like me to give you a tour?" Maybe if she got him alone in a room, her nerves would settle. His eyes were kind, but she couldn't detect any spark of interest there at all. Just...friendliness. *Ew.*

"Thanks, but I've already had one. I met with Draper the other day about moving some of my investments. He showed me around."

"But...but now it's fully furnished! We installed the artwork yesterday, and I can show you the Remington sculpture—"

"I have an appointment with Draper next week, so I'll see it then. If you'll excuse me, I see a friend of mine over by the carving station." And he walked away, joined by his brother. Belle had a sneaky suspicion it had nothing to do with *seeing a friend* either.

"Smooth." Savannah's voice was dry. "You're about as subtle as a heart attack. Why are you putting on this Scarlett O'Hara routine with Stefan? All fluttery and desperate."

"Oh, shut up." Belle pouted, folding her arms.

"I felt a connection with him at the weddings on New Year's Eve, and he's a Mendoza, so…"

"Ah, the old Mendozas marry Fortunes thing. You know that's not a law, right?"

"Says the Fortune who married a Mendoza."

Her sister's face softened, and she slid her arm over Belle's shoulders. "The sister who fell in *love* with a man who happens to have the last name Mendoza. It wasn't predetermined. And that's how *you'll* fall in love, sweetie. It'll happen when you least expect it. And definitely *not* while you're trying to drag some poor Mendoza man to look at a sculpture." Savannah gave her shoulders a squeeze. "Besides, didn't I see you kissing that hunky brother of Harper's last weekend?"

"Jack? That was…nothing." Which was a lie. That kiss was *something*. "Between you and me— and I will kill you if you say a word to anyone else—Jack offered to help me make Stefan jealous. The kiss was an act."

Savannah was silent for a moment.

"Really? An act, huh? And he offered to…" A weird expression crossed Savannah's face, then vanished. Amusement? Curiosity? It was gone before Belle could define it. Savannah was a scientist, so her mind worked a little differently from other people—she analyzed things endlessly.

"Well, that's an interesting plan. And speak of the devil…"

Belle turned to see Jack coming in with Harper and Brady. He'd followed her suggestion, wearing what looked to be brand-new dark charcoal jeans, Western boots and a black sport coat over a white shirt left open at the neck. His gaze found her almost immediately. No visible smile, of course— that wasn't Jack's thing. But his eyes warmed and the creases around them relaxed.

Savannah muttered something under her breath. Belle looked up and her sister shrugged. "This little plan of yours might just work. You should try a little harder and maybe Stefan will notice." Jack was heading their way now.

"You think so?"

"Oh, yeah. I definitely think you and Jack should spend more time together. I mean, you may as well have some fun with it." Savannah pressed her lips together. The way she did when she was trying not to laugh. Before Belle could question it, her sister greeted Jack, then walked away to join her husband and Stefan. She looked back and gave Belle a thumbs-up gesture behind Jack's back.

"Look at us, dressing like twinsies." He gestured at her suit. "I gotta say, you wear it better."

"I don't know." She smiled up at him. "You look very cowboy chic."

"And you…" He leaned back to look at her again, a smile teasing his mouth. "You look like a calendar girl for Hot Office Workers. That skirt is…" His smile appeared in full. "Let's just say Mendoza can't ignore you in that."

She had a feeling Stefan hadn't paid attention to her outfit at all.

"We talked for a few minutes, but he…um…had to go talk business with my brothers. He's moving his accounts here."

"Ooh…" Jack winked playfully. "That'll give you plenty of chances to see him. Are you sure you need me hanging around?"

"Yes, absolutely." She surprised herself. She didn't technically *need* him, but she didn't like the thought of him not being at her side. "I mean…it can't hurt the Mendoza situation, and let's face it— we're both new in town. If we stick together for a while, we won't have to keep going places alone."

"Makes sense." He put his arm around her waist and tugged her close. "We'll have to really sell this if we want to resolve the *Mendoza situation*."

His hand on her hip made Belle's pulse go hot and quick. Determined not to show how he'd affected her, she raised her chin and slid her arm under his jacket. Did his eyes just go a shade darker? From mahogany to espresso? They stood, staring at each other. She realized she wasn't all nervous and loud and fake with Jack, the way she had been with Stefan. While *relaxed* didn't exactly describe how his embrace made her feel, she was comfortable with him. Oddly familiar.

"Well, if we're going to sell it…" She tipped her head back and rose on her toes. He didn't hesitate to put his hand behind her head and kiss her. It was a soft kiss. Not as showy as the one in the ballroom. But his lips moving against hers made her feel like her insides were melting all the same. He lifted his head and stared hard into her eyes.

"Maybe you should show me around." His voice was gravelly and low. "Maybe to a quiet office somewhere?"

Going to a quiet office meant only one thing. More kissing. In private. Which wasn't the point of their playacting. She grabbed his hand anyway and led him down the hallway to Beau's office. Savannah told her to have fun, right?

The only light in the room was the light on Beau's desk. She closed the door behind them and turned, only to have Jack press her against the door, his hands gripping her shoulders. He paused with his mouth inches from hers, searching her face.

"I want to be clear here, Belle. For just a few minutes, I need to *not* be acting with you. I need to not be thinking of who might see. I need to not be thinking of that freakin' Mendoza guy. When I kiss you, I…" His fingers loosened, as if he'd realized how tightly he'd been holding her. "I need us to be Jack and Belle…kissing each other's lights out."

Her insides quivered like a tuning fork, and she barely whispered her answer.

"Yes, please."

The hiss of the word was still on her lips when his mouth crashed into hers. No need for genteel kisses in here—their heads turned and their tongues fought and their teeth clicked together as desire took charge. He had one large hand on her butt cheek and the other behind her head, lifting her and pressing his hard body against her. She entwined her arms around his neck, desperate to get closer. He spun and placed her on the desk, cupping her face now with both hands. The only sound in the room was their panting breaths and an occasional groan as the kiss went on and on.

Jack pulled away first, suddenly stepping back and turning away, jamming his hands through his brown hair. "Holy… We gotta stop. We can't do this. Not here. That would be a really bad idea."

She braced her hands behind her and leaned back, crossing her legs tightly to ease the tingling heat between them. She grinned at Jack.

"Are you talking to me or yourself?"

He huffed out a laugh. "Both." He turned to look at her. "Someone could walk in here any minute now. And you want...you want something else. Some*one* else."

Right now Belle only wanted Jack's hands on her again. His mouth on hers again. She'd never felt this kind of burning need before.

"Jack, that other plan might never work. And in the meantime we could..." She grimaced. "Does that make me sound slutty?"

He shook his head with a chagrined smile. "Nope. We're both adults. But you don't strike me as a woman who'd be sneaking off for kisses with one guy while hoping to date another. We need to figure out what we're doing. With our brains..." He tapped the side of his head. "Not our hormones. I think maybe we should cool this until we do."

She sat up and slid off the desk. Her *brother's* desk. A minute ago, she'd have let Jack do whatever he wanted on that desk. He was right. They were making decisions based on...heat. She didn't come to Texas for hot sex on a desk. Her hand slid across the top of the desk. She sure had been tempted. She lifted her chin, feeling more in control with Jack a few feet away.

"You're right, of course. Like I said, we're both new in town without knowing a lot of other people. It makes sense that we'd be attracted to each other, but taking this any further would probably be a bad idea."

"Probably." He stared at the floor for a minute. "We should knock off the kissing because…"

"Because we clearly can't control ourselves?"

"Yeah." Jack rubbed the back of his neck and sighed. "I'm not sure why that happens, but it can't lead to anything good. Not with the Mendoza situation still in play."

What if she gave up on the Mendoza situation? What then? No. She wasn't here for a fling. She was here to find a husband, damn it. They stared at each other. *Damn it.*

Jack took her hand in his and turned for the door. "Let's get back before people notice we snuck off together."

She reluctantly agreed, following him back to the now-crowded cocktail party. He was a perfect gentleman the rest of the evening, staying by her side, smiling softly on occasion. Once in a while he'd rest his hand on her waist, but never for long. It was as if it burned him, and she understood. His fingers burned her, too. She tried to quench the fire with wine. It didn't work at first, but she didn't give up. She was no quitter.

Pretty soon she was giggling at everything anyone said, and people seemed to be giggling at her, too. She knew she was buzzed, but at least she was starting to relax. Jack was never too far away. She'd shared a few words with Stefan, but they were inconsequential and always with other people around. Polite conversation about the cool weather moving in and something about something happening at the winery. Belle wasn't really listening. A few minutes after that, Jack handed her a glass of water.

"Your eyes are getting a little fuzzy, princess."

Funny, he didn't look fuzzy at all. He looked delicious. She gave herself a mental shake. No. Jack said they were a bad idea. Just because his kisses sent her up in flames—that didn't *mean* anything. That was physical. It wasn't real.

Jack really wished Belle would stop looking at him like that. Like she felt the same hunger he did. Every time he caught himself staring back into those ocean-blue eyes of hers, he had to remind himself of the Mendoza situation. She only wanted Jack around to catch the attention of another man, even though that man was too blind to see her the way Jack did.

An older woman walked up, her bright blond hair brushing her shoulders. She wore a sweeping long skirt and a lacy cream-colored blouse. She introduced herself and Belle's eyes went wide.

"Oh, my gosh, you're *the* Mariana from Mariana's Market? Oh, I love that place! Last week I bought a turquoise-studded belt from one of your vendors that I can't wait to wear."

Mariana complimented Belle's bright blue earrings, and the fashion conversation took off from there. Jack was content just to be near Belle. There weren't a lot of things that made him feel content these days.

Sure, he was glad to be living near his sister and her new family. He was relieved to have a job. And Callum had even mentioned that he might have a rental house available, if Jack was willing to do some sweat equity in the place. Which wasn't a problem. He had plenty of energy to burn off. He watched as Belle laughed at something Mariana said. She'd drained the large glass of water quickly, and between that and the fashion talk, her eyes were already more clear. She caught him watching her and grinned before turning back to Mariana. Yes, this was contentment he felt.

He'd felt a lot more than that in her brother's office. When he thought of how close they'd come to clearing that desk and— He called a halt to those thoughts and reminded himself what he was doing. *Mendoza situation. Mendoza situation.* His body relaxed again as he forced himself to stop thinking about the way her lips felt on his. The way her

legs had wrapped around his. The way... *Aw hell...
Mendoza situation!*

"...barbecue on Sunday around two. Why don't
you join us?"

Jack blinked, realizing that his brother-in-law
was standing beside him and talking to him. Good.
A distraction. Was it warm in here?

"Earth to Jack." His sister snapped her fingers
in his face, making him flinch.

"Yeah, yeah, I'm here. Sunday sounds good.
What do you want me to bring?"

Harper rolled her eyes. "Why? Are you going
to whip something up in that little hotel room of
yours? You don't even have a kitchenette, do you?"

"No, but I'm perfectly capable of buying something. A bottle of wine? A dessert?"

"Wine would be great," Brady said. "Whatever
vintage goes with burgers."

"So how long are you going to stay at the
hotel?" Harper fixed him with a hard stare. "Isn't
that getting expensive? Have you looked at houses
yet? You have a job now, right?"

Brady cautioned his wife. "Honey, take it easy
on the guy." He looked at Jack. "I need a refill.
You want another beer?"

"Nah, I'm good." Belle had taken another glass
of wine from one of the servers still wandering
around with trays, and he wanted to be sober

enough to drive her back to the hotel if necessary. Brady left Jack with Harper, who had no intention of letting go of her big sister role.

"Is the job going okay? Is it a job you think you'll be happy with?"

"I've had the job for three days, Harper, but yeah. It's good." Callum seemed pleased with the job he'd done at the veterinary clinic and had assigned him to a crew working on some homes they were building outside town. Apparently doing residential construction was a change of gears for the company. Callum had explained it was part of their promise to be more involved in the Rambling Rose community—not only bringing jobs, but providing more housing options as well.

"Jack…" Harper's voice was low. "Is it the transition to civilian life that has you so closed up? You're not yourself."

He blew out a long sigh. "I'm me, Harper. What you see is…me. The only me I know how to be right now. I don't know what you want."

"I want my brother back." Her voice broke, and he reached out to touch her arm while she continued, "You don't laugh anymore. You barely even smile. I want the guy who used to loosen the top on the saltshaker, or put salt in the sugar bowl. The guy who rubbed charcoal on the binoculars before you handed them to me at Niagara Falls, then didn't tell me I was walking around looking like a raccoon for an hour afterward."

His mouth twitched at that memory. He'd tortured his sister on a regular basis. "Are you saying you want me to act like I did when I was fourteen? Aren't we a little old for that, sis? You've got three kids. I've been—"

"You've been to war and back." Harper put her hand over his, gripping his fingers. "And you won't tell me anything about it. All I know is you got some medal for something. Probably something stupidly heroic and dangerous. But you won't talk about it."

"Sis…" He tried to reassure her. "A lot of soldiers don't talk about what they do or see over there. Most of the days are boring as hell, and the days that aren't boring…well…it's not exactly cocktail party conversation. But I'm okay. As for that medal…I never should have mentioned it in my emails to you. I didn't deserve it, and I don't want to discuss it, okay?"

The last words came out as a plea. She gave him a sad smile, and her voice softened.

"I'm sorry to push. You know me—I worry." She reached up and rearranged his hair, which he suspected was probably wild from his adventure with Belle earlier. "Just know that I'm here for you. Whenever you're ready."

He nodded, his throat suddenly thick with emotion. It took some effort to swallow it. "I know, Harper. I promise if I need to talk, I'll be at your door." He grinned and tugged a strand of her hair. "I'll also be at your door for burgers on Sunday."

He looked around and realized he'd let Belle escape his line of vision. He frowned. Had she left? Was she driving after all that wine? Had she and Mendoza…? No, Stefan was in the corner talking with a group of people. Jack excused himself from his sister and started searching, trying to quell the weird sense of panic rising in him.

"Looking for Tinkerbelle?" a woman asked him, a wry smile on her face. It took him a second to place her. She was Belle's older sister, Savannah. She didn't wait for him to answer. "There's a Fortune poker game going on down the hall, and my brother Beau dared her to try to beat our cousin Callum. She's basically a poker savant. Mainly because she counts cards." Why was this woman he barely knew telling him all this? She nodded down the hall. "Go on—there are a bunch of guys down there. And Belle's probably cleaning out our cousins' wallets." A sharp gleam appeared in her eyes. "They're in Beau's office. You know where that is, right?"

Uh-oh.

"Um…" No sense pretending. Clearly she knew.

Jack didn't know if she'd seen them or if Belle told her. "Last door on the left?"

He could hear Savannah laughing behind him as he walked down the hall. There were voices ahead of him, then a burst of curse words, groans and laughter. The laughter was Belle's. He got to the doorway and froze. Guys were sitting in chairs or on the floor around a coffee table—Callum and Kane in armchairs, Beau and Draper on the floor. Chaz Mendoza, Belle's brother-in-law, was leaning against the same desk Jack had deposited Belle on a couple hours earlier.

She was on the low leather sofa. She'd kicked off her shoes, her bare feet tucked under herself, hiking the already short skirt even higher on her thighs. Her jacket was off, tossed on the back of the sofa. The satiny camisole barely covered her, held up with tiny spaghetti straps. Her hair, which had been loose, was now held up on top of her head with a metal binder clip from the desk. Still laughing, she leaned forward and scooped the pile of dollar bills off the table and onto the pile already at her side. She looked up and gave him a huge smile and wave.

"Hey, it's Jack! Guys, you've met Jack, right?" She giggled. She was drunk. And adorable. "Oh, of course you have. Callum's your boss, right? Are you here to take me on or take me home?"

Both options sounded good to him. "If you want a ride back to the hotel, I'm happy to oblige." He caught the protectiveness in her brothers' expressions and raised his hands. "I'm going there anyway. She shouldn't drive."

"*She* is sitting right here." Belle sat up and pulled on her jacket. "I've beaten these suckers out of enough money. And you're right about the driving thing." She weaved a bit as she stood and Draper rose and took her arm. She swatted him away. "I'm perfectly capable of walking unaided."

"I'll drive you back, sis," Draper said.

Savannah walked in just then. "Draper, stop trying to act like Daddy. Belle's safe with Jack." She looked back at him. "Right?"

"Yes, ma'am."

Savannah shuddered. "Oh, God—don't call me *ma'am*. I feel old enough these days."

He grinned. "Okay. But she *is* safe with me." The real question was whether or not he was safe around *her*.

Belle was in rare form all the way back to the hotel. Flirty and talkative, she bragged about beating her cousins at poker, then her mood took a sharp turn and she stared out the window, talking to herself more than him.

"I'm their fun little parlor trick."

"Excuse me?"

"Numbers are my thing." She sounded melancholy. "I'm good at cards because I'm good at math. I know my odds. I know what cards are out there, which ones are still in the deck. I do numbers off the top of my head." She twisted in the seat. "Ask me any math equation. Multiplication. Division. Percentages. Make it weird, though. Not 10 percent of a thousand or anything silly."

"Okay." He squinted. "What's 35 percent of 6,345?"

"2,200."

Her answer came so fast it made him laugh. "Damn, girl. You *are* good."

"Come on. A 30-something percent of a number starting with six? Kid's stuff. Give me something harder."

He parked and they headed toward the hotel entrance. She was still barefoot, her shoes dangling from her fingers. They were waiting for the elevator when he finally answered her.

"Fine. What's 42 percent of 13,562?"

She had to think about that one. For about three seconds.

"Fifty-seven hundred, give or take a few digits."

The elevator stopped on her floor—the top floor, of course. She stumbled a little, and he grabbed her elbow. "I honestly have no idea, but I don't doubt that you're right. That's amazing."

"Yep. That's my parlor trick."

"Belle…" He took her arm and waited for her to make eye contact, even if her focus was a little off. He needed her to hear this. "Your talents are more than a parlor trick." He bit back his irritation with her brothers for making her feel that way, whether they meant to or not. "You're an intelligent woman with mad math skills. Don't let anyone, not even your family, make you feel otherwise." Her eyes welled up with tears. Hoo-boy, she was tipsy *and* weepy. She blinked at the key card in her hand like she didn't know what it was. He took it from her and opened the door to her suite. "Did you eat tonight?"

She marched into the room ahead of him with a dramatic sigh. "I was too busy to eat."

That explained both her emotional state and her level of intoxication.

"I'll order some food to be brought up." He opened the refrigerator—the suite had a full kitchen—and handed her a bottle of water to drink in the meantime.

She took it and sat on the edge of the sofa. He was glad she had the suite, because the bed was out of sight. He didn't need that temptation when she was clearly in no shape to make decisions. He picked up the phone and ordered a toasted cheese and tomato sandwich with chips and a slice of pound cake. Nothing too spicy or rich. He paced the room while he waited. He was afraid she'd fall asleep before room service got there.

"This is a nice suite."

She looked around and wrinkled her nose. "It's home for now. It's nice, but getting a little claustrophobic." She drained the water bottle and he handed her another. Her eyes were a bit clearer already. "I miss my things."

There was a framed picture of a rose on the desk. The rose was done in watercolor, and the frame was made of ornate silver. He picked it up, surprised how heavy it was. It didn't look like hotel decor. "Family heirloom?"

"No, but it's pretty, isn't it?" She stood and came to his side. "It was in my room when I got here, in a white box with my name on it. I figured it was a wedding favor, but I mentioned it to a few people who were at the wedding, and no one else got anything like it. Maybe I have a secret admirer."

Jack didn't like the sound of that. He turned the frame over and noticed a small inscription on the back of the frame.

A rose by any other name would smell as sweet—MAF

It didn't sound like anything threatening. Jack said it looked more like a housewarming or welcome gift, and Belle agreed.

"Between the rose and the inscription, it has to be something to do with Rambling Rose. I figure the *MAF* is the artist's initials."

There was a discreet knock at the door. Jack took the tray and tipped the woman who'd delivered it. He set it on the tiny table and Belle sat to eat.

"Before you go to bed, you should take some aspirin," he told her, giving her his hangover remedy.

Her flirtatious side appeared again, and she gave him a wink. "You aren't going to stay?"

Oh, boy, did he want to. He calmly declined and left her there, knowing he was going to need a long, cold shower when he got to his room. Belle wasn't one-night-stand material. And he wasn't looking for a relationship. And the biggest obstacle of all?

She wanted someone else.

Chapter Six

"So let me get this straight…" Meg stared wide-eyed over the rim of her coffee mug. "You and this Jack guy were *acting*, then you snuck away and *stopped* acting and it was…hot. Then you decided not to do that again. And now…he's asking you for decorating advice?"

Belle and Meg were in a local coffee shop, Kirby's Perks. Meg was co-owner of Roja and Provisions, but she told Belle she found this cozy coffee shop relaxing because she was just a customer there. Some of the regulars were there that morning—a woman with red hair sitting in the corner typing rapidly on her laptop and an elderly bearded gentleman by the window.

"Well, style *is* the business I want to be in." She took her last bite of cinnamon muffin, wishing there was more of it. "Not home decorating, but…style. Design. Art. Ideas."

"In his *house*. After you both promised no more kissy stuff." Meg raised a brow. "You're going to Jack's *house*."

Meg was the only person—other than Savannah—who knew what Belle and Jack were doing. Even though Stefan Mendoza was Meg's brother-in-law, she'd vowed to keep Belle's secret.

Going to Jack's new rental house might be a little risky. But she and Jack had agreed the night of the party to turn down the heat. They were adults and perfectly capable of doing that. She hoped. She'd been tipsy and silly at the party. She'd flirted. Hard. She'd wanted another one of those scorching kisses. But he'd turned her down. At least *one* of them could be responsible.

She looked across the table to Meg. "He and I agreed to behave. And we've both started our jobs now, so we're not running into each other. And he's moved out of the hotel, so…that's that."

Meg's head tipped to the side. "Again…you're going to his *house*."

"I offered to help the guy. As a friend!"

Meg straightened abruptly. "You *offered*? You made it sound like he asked you."

"Did I?" Belle shrugged. Maybe Meg was the wrong person to tell. But she'd been bursting to talk to someone. Savannah knew about her and Jack, but her sister was hardly an impartial listener. She'd been taking way too much delight in Belle's situation. So she'd trusted Meg. She forgot what a stickler she was for details.

"Uh, yeah. You definitely made it sound like it was his idea. How did you end up offering your… um…services?"

It had happened innocently enough. She and Jack sometimes saw each other at breakfast at the hotel, and he'd walked over a few days ago and told her he'd rented a house from Callum, paying part of the rent in labor updating the place. He told her the house was built in the late 1980s and never remodeled. It was apparently awash in mauve paint, lots of wallpaper and shiny brass fixtures. She had a hard time imagining a guy like Jack living in a rose pink house, so she'd offered to give him some help picking new paint colors. As a friend.

"As a friend…" Meg repeated. "I'm beginning to wonder about that."

Belle grimaced. "There might be a little chemistry between Jack and me, but we're handling it. Besides, I'm bored out of my mind these days."

Meg's brows rose. "Bored? Aren't you working all day every day now?"

"You're forgetting the one difference between us, Meg." Belle smiled her thanks at Kirby, the owner of the coffee shop, for refilling her coffee. "You actually enjoy moving numbers around. Now that the office is open and I'm back into the daily grind of it, I'm getting more and more restless to do my own thing."

"Belle's Boutique? Didn't you promise your brothers a year at Fortune Investments?"

"I did. I don't want to leave them in the lurch, but I can't help thinking about how exciting and challenging it would be to get my *own* business off the ground." She took a sip of coffee and sighed. "Shopping for myself every weekend is getting old." She grinned. "You haven't known me long enough to know how unusual it is for me to ever say that shopping is boring. Helping Jack will let me stretch my creative muscles a little."

Meg didn't answer right away. "I get what you're saying but—" she winked playfully "—I have a feeling some other muscles in your body are looking to get stretched with Jack Radcliffe."

Of course, Belle denied it. Meg was probably no more convinced of her sincerity than Belle was.

Jack leaned back in the folding chair on the spacious—and mostly empty—veranda and watched his three-legged dog run around the fenced yard. For a guy who believed in strategic planning, the past week had been a whirlwind of impulsive decisions.

When Callum offered to show him some houses he'd purchased in this older neighborhood, hoping to improve, then flip them, he'd given Jack his pick of three vacant ones to live in while remodeling it. This four-bedroom gray brick ranch at the end of the cul-de-sac was way too much house for a single guy. Especially a single guy who didn't own a stick of furniture. But the minute he'd seen the huge fenced-in yard, all he'd been able to hear were Stephanie's words at the veterinary clinic.

...he needs a home with a big, fenced yard where he can run and play...

The last thing Jack needed was a big house and lawn to care for. Or a dog. But Sarge needed a home, damn it. Callum hadn't tried to hide his surprise when Jack said he'd take the cul-de-sac house. And Stephanie had been even more thrilled when he'd shown up at the clinic to claim Sarge.

And Sarge? Well, Sarge didn't know what to do with himself. He'd scampered to every corner of the house last night, sniffing each inch. Jack thought the dog's eyes were going to pop right out of his head cartoon-style when he let him out in the yard for the first time. The lot was deep and wedge shaped, with two live oaks to offer shade and the remnants of what was once some formal landscaping along the fence line and around the veranda.

The dog was investigating under every bush and shrub right now, his stub of a tail wriggling in pure joy. Jack was surprised that tail hadn't just fallen right off at this point—it hadn't stopped wriggling since Sarge arrived. He was one happy dog. And he'd already made Jack a little bit happier, too. He heard the doorbell and left the dog to explore.

Belle was waiting on his front porch when the door swung open. Her hair was loose, which he'd decided was his favorite look on her. Even if it was impractical for painting. And speaking of impractical... Was she wearing *heels*? They were cork wedges—a term he only knew because of his sister—and were at least five inches high. She was in jeans, but they were white. And her loose-knit sweater was white, too, although he could see a bright blue tank top underneath. As always, she looked fabulous, but...

"You *do* know we're painting today, right?"

Her brows gathered. "We're *picking* paint today. Shopping for paint colors."

"No." He shook his head. "I mean, we are doing that, but then we're coming back to put it on the walls. Or at least I am. Looks like you'll be supervising. When you offered to help, I thought—"

"I offered to help with design. Not execution."

She leaned to peek inside. "Are you going to ask me in or not?" He stepped to the side and she swept by him. The woman was five foot two inches of pure attitude. "The landscaping looks like a jungle out front. And— Wow." She stopped and looked around the huge, empty great room. "That's a lot of mauve. And…is that a mirrored wall?"

Jack winced. "I'm afraid so, but it'll be coming down soon. And the carpeting will be coming up. Callum's sending over a crew to handle the big projects. If you think this is bad, wait until you see the kitchen."

He led the way and Belle started laughing. He couldn't blame her. The pale cupboards had ceramic roses for handles. The counters were a dark, dusky rose. The floor was the same color, but in hexagon tiles. The walls were covered in wallpaper with roses on it. The brass light hanging over the breakfast nook had—of course—pink roses on it. But at least the kitchen layout was workable, once he de-pinked it.

Belle stood in the center of the room. "This is… I don't even know what to say. The pink is…" She shook her head, as if that would change what she was seeing. "It's a lot. What made you rent something so huge? Do you have a secret family and five children I don't know about?"

He snorted a chuckle, rolling his eyes.

"No secret family. Callum got a great deal on it and wants to fix it up and sell it eventually. I made a deal that I'll work on updating it for a break in my rent. Most of the work is cosmetic."

"Maybe, but there's so much work." She walked back through the arched opening to the great room, with its soaring cathedral ceilings. "When does your furniture arrive?"

There wasn't a stick of furniture in the great room. Or most of the rest of the house.

"I just got out of the Army, remember?"

"Well, yeah, but…this place is empty."

"No. There's a breakfast set." There was a glass-topped metal table with black metal chairs around it.

"That's *patio* furniture." Belle pointed. "There's even a hole in it for an umbrella."

"Right now it's my dining table."

"Do you at least have a bed?"

"Sort of. I have a mattress and box spring on a frame." He splayed his hands. "Belle, I don't need a lot. And there's no sense putting any furniture in the rooms before I pull up this carpeting and paint, right?"

There was a blur of movement outside the floor-to-ceiling windows, and Belle let out a squeal of fright. "What was that? Oh, my God, was that some wild animal?" She looked around the room as if she expected giant rats to appear. He chuckled.

"That's my dog."

Belle went to the window. "Is that *Sarge*?"

Not only had she remembered the dog that brought them together, she remembered his name.

"It is. They said he needed a place with a big, fenced yard. When I saw the yard here, I—"

"So you rented this house for a dog."

Belle wasn't sure what to do with all the feelings that welled up inside her. Jack didn't answer, but she knew she was right. He moved into this huge, tired house because a three-legged dog needed a place to run. Jack was a pretty closed-up guy. His smile was elusive, and his laughter was rarely more than a chuckle that he probably wished he could hold in. Despite that, she knew he was a good guy. But to actually see that goodness in action took her breath away. She blinked and looked around, then laughed at him in amazement.

"This is the fanciest doghouse I've ever seen!"

There was a glint of definite humor in his eyes. "Are you saying my dog is spoiled already?"

She patted Jack's chest absently. "I'm saying you're an old softy. You can hide that big heart from everyone else, Jack Radcliffe, but *I* know your secret now. You're a big marshmallow."

She hadn't realized that her hand was still resting on his chest until he covered it with his own and held it there against his shirt. She could feel his heart beating strong and steady beneath her fingers. She gulped and looked up through her lashes, feeling a flood of emotion that had nothing to do with him being a nice man.

"You don't know all my secrets." His voice was low. More intense than she expected. "But you do have a way of wiggling past my defenses." They stared at each other for a beat before he released her and stepped back and cleared his throat. "But you're not going to distract me from the work that needs to be done. First we'll go to the paint store, then we'll come back and start painting the bedroom and master bathroom. I think the bathroom will be fine with paint and new fixtures. There's a lot of neutral white marble in there."

When she followed him into the master suite, she understood what he meant. The walls were, like everything else in the house, pink, with one accent wall of dark cranberry. It didn't strike her as Jack's style at all.

"I don't mind pink in general—" Belle wrinkled her nose "—but this house is seriously over the top. Getting this room under control will at least give you a refuge until we can get the rest painted."

"That was my thought, too. We have to start somewhere."

He brought Sarge inside, and the dog about lost his mind with happiness when he discovered Belle. She knelt on the floor to hug him as he jumped all over her.

"He gets around so great with only one front leg. Do they know what happened?"

Jack knelt on one knee and scratched Sarge's head. "They found him along the road. They don't know if he was hit by a car or if someone kicked him, but the break was too high to set." Jack looked at her, his eyes soft and solemn. "Pit bulls are hard to place, and one with three legs is even harder. He deserves to have a home like a normal dog."

"I agree." There was that flood of emotion again. "He doesn't seem to miss the leg at all."

Jack nodded, reaching for her hand and standing, pulling her up with him. He pointed to the crate nearby, and Sarge hopped in obediently, curling up on the bedding inside. "Stephanie said animals don't react to stuff the way humans do. They tend to accept things that happen as just… life. They adjust and move on, without stressing about what they've lost. Sarge figured out how to move as a tripod, and that's his life now."

"That acceptance is a skill a lot of humans could use."

They went to the paint store, and she convinced Jack that a warm charcoal gray could replace the dark red wall, and then a silver gray for the lighter walls. It would make the rooms feel contemporary, and could be softened with artwork and furniture. When he *had* furniture.

They stopped at a Tex-Mex food truck for fajitas for lunch and two orders of chili to reheat later. When they got to the house, he let Sarge out back and they sat on the veranda to eat. Jack let out a soft moan at his first bite of the steak fajita and Belle grinned over at him.

"Didn't get too many of these in the military, huh?"

"They definitely didn't show up on the chow line overseas." He took another bite. "And if they had, they'd have been awful." He swallowed. "This is the opposite of awful."

"How long were you over there?"

"Which time? I did two tours. One was eleven months. The last was fifteen."

"Where were you stationed? Afghanistan?"

There was the slightest shift in Jack's demeanor. Hard to define, but she felt the chill from it.

"My first tour was Afghanistan. This last one was Iraq. I wasn't *stationed.* I was deployed."

"Okay. What did you do there?" She didn't know many veterans. Her friend Shelly's brother and father had both served but they'd rarely talked about it.

"What did I do?" His eyes went flat. "Nothing good."

Belle knew combat could be traumatic. She'd heard about PTSD. Maybe that was why Jack was so closed up? But he didn't seem to be traumatized in any way. He was always calm. Always in control. Amused, even if he wasn't exactly jolly. He didn't want to talk about his time in the military, but that didn't mean he was suffering because of it.

"You don't want to talk about it, do you?"

"No offense, but…no. I don't. Besides, we have work to do." He stood and scanned her white outfit with a sigh. "I guess this is where you skedaddle. You can't paint in that."

"Says who?" She kicked off her platform sandals and peeled off her sweater, tossing it on the chair she'd just vacated. "These jeans are old. So is this top." She tugged at the tank. "I'm not afraid of a little paint." She reached in her pocket for a hair scrunchie, pulled her loose hair up high on her head. "Let's go."

She knew Jack thought she was some sort of diva. She liked style and bling, and as a Fortune, she had money. But she worked hard for the family business, and it wasn't her fault if her parents gave each child a little help early in life rather than waiting for an inheritance.

But after four hours of painting in the bedroom— with that king-size mattress sitting right there—she dared him to call her a diva. She'd managed to get two coats of paint on all three lighter walls, while he'd put three heavy coats of steel gray on the dark wall. The pink was gone—in here, at least. She walked to the bathroom door and shook her head.

"We'll never get this done tonight."

Jack walked up behind her, draping his arm over her shoulder. "It definitely won't get done before dinner. I might work on it later, though. But first, chili burgers." She followed his eyes down her body, her clothes splattered with silver paint. He grimaced. "I owe you new jeans."

"No you don't. These are very chic now...especially if I add a few rips and tears to them." He was paint splattered, too. She reached up to pick some out of his hair and laughed. "I forget how tall you are until I'm standing here in my bare feet."

Jack tapped the tip of her nose. "Maybe what you're forgetting is how short *you* are."

The air was suddenly charged with electricity. That happened whenever his fingers touched her skin. What would happen if they hopped into that bed right there behind him? *What? No.* They'd agreed to no more kissing. And definitely no hopping into beds! She started to give him a flippant answer, but the doorbell rang before she could. They heard the door swing wide and Jack's sister call out.

"Jack! We brought food! And children!" Jack muttered a curse under his breath. They could hear small feet echoing as they pounded around the great room. "Jack?"

"Be right there, sis!" he called out, giving Belle an oddly disappointed look. Had he been thinking about that bed, too? "I forgot she said she might stop by. I definitely didn't expect a family invasion. Guess those chili burgers will have to wait until tomorrow."

She followed him out of the bedroom, chewing her lip to keep from smiling. He'd said *tomorrow* as if he expected her to be there.

Chapter Seven

Harper's mouth slid from a bright smile into a perfect circle of surprise when she spotted Belle. Then it slid right back into a smile again. One filled with speculation and laughter. Jack should have known his sister wouldn't wait long to scope out his new home.

"Belle!" Harper nearly shouted the word, making baby Christina startle in the carrier strapped to her chest before she settled again at her mom's touch. "I'm sorry if we…um…interrupted anything. You said you'd be painting, and I didn't know your kitchen situation yet and—" Harper looked around. "Where is your furniture?"

Belle started to laugh behind him, and he turned
to soak it in. Her laughter had a way of shooting
through his armor and making him feel...lighter.

"You didn't interrupt anything," Belle said,
stepping up to his side. "We were just attacking
all the pink in this place. I'm taking Jack furniture
shopping tomorrow." His brows rose. She was? "It
should look a little more like a home by the end
of the week. Let's take the food out back." She
glanced up at Jack, her voice dropping. "Is Sarge
okay with kids?"

He nodded in response, taking one of the bags
from Brady. "Steph said he's great with kids, but
we should still introduce them first." Toby and
Tyler were already standing at the big windows
facing the back. "Can you boys be calm when you
meet the dog?"

Brady chuckled. "Doubtful, but we'll see."

They went out to the veranda. The boys were
surprisingly sweet with Sarge, petting him and solemnly introducing themselves as if they'd taken
Jack's request literally. As for Sarge, he immediately rolled over to present his belly for scratching,
tongue lolling out of his mouth as the boys obliged.

Sarge was thrilled to see company, and as soon
as Toby tossed a tennis ball, Sarge charged after
it. Soon the dog and the boys were exploring the
big yard together as the adults set out dinner on

the huge teak picnic table that had come with the house.

Harper had stopped at Provisions for a Mediterranean dish of sautéed chicken and eggplant over rice with Greek salads, and homemade cookies for dessert. Brady brought beer and a bottle of wine, and Belle played hostess, finding the paper plates and plastic utensils he'd stocked the kitchen with. Belle gave Harper and Brady a tour of the house after dinner, while Jack kept an eye on the boys and the dog. Sarge eventually curled up at Jack's feet, exhausted, leaving the boys to play alone. Within minutes, they were up on one of the lower limbs of the oak trees, staring over the fence to the expanse of prairie behind the development. The sun was setting and lit the sky and prairie in pinks and gold.

Harper sat next to him and poured herself a glass of wine. "This is quite a view. It's a big house, Jack. And you have a dog." She looked down at Sarge. "Is he helping?"

Jack lifted an eyebrow. "He's not much of a painter, so…"

"Is he helping *you*? Is *any* of this helping? The dog? The house that's really a giant project? That paint-spattered woman?"

"Helping what, sis?" He didn't want to talk about it, but he didn't want to be alone with it either. It was weird. His head was often in a weird place these days.

"Someday you'll have to snap out of it and tell the truth about whatever's going on with you." Harper took a sip of wine. "In the meantime, I hope the dog, this ridiculous house and especially the woman... Well, I hope they help you."

A comfortable silence settled over them as they watched the sun settle low on the horizon. Brady and Belle joined them, and Brady went straight out to help the boys down from the tree. Harper explained one of the boys had broken his arm falling from a tree last year.

Belle continued playing hostess, clearing the table and making coffee. When she brought the coffeepot out to the veranda, she fixed him with an exasperated look.

"You and I are *definitely* going shopping, boy. Styrofoam cups? Seriously?" She held up the stack of cups. "First, they're horrible for the environment. Second, they make coffee taste like plastic. And third, they're just plain tacky."

When his sister and her family were leaving later, Harper leaned in to whisper in Jack's ear. "Oh, yeah, she's good for you."

He almost whispered back, *"She wants someone else,"* but choked it down. Belle left shortly after, promising they had a full day coming up in the morning. Jack stared at Sarge, asking the dog what the hell he was getting himself into. Sarge just wagged his tail, walked into his crate and collapsed on the bedding, done for the day.

Jack had been nervous that Belle was going to take him to some swanky store on Sunday. She might think he had a Fortune's bank account. But the first question she'd asked when they drove to Austin the next morning was "What's your budget?" He told her and she directed him to a furniture outlet. "That much should take care of the great room and your bedroom if we're careful with it, and we'll be able to stock the kitchen, too."

He was skeptical, but dang if she didn't manage to do it. She knew exactly what she wanted and how much she wanted to pay for it. The salesman learned to just follow her orders, like Jack was doing. And it was all stuff he actually liked.

Next up was the giant box store, where they loaded two carts with housewares and a mountain of other items he hadn't even thought about. And food, too.

The entire time, the two of them talked about a million things that had nothing to do with shopping—favorite movies, books, podcasts, games. Her brothers' business, her role there, her dream of opening a boutique. They were almost back to Rambling Rose by the time that topic came up.

"Why did you take the job with Beau and Draper if what you really want is your own business?"

She stared out the window for a moment. "When they asked me to come to Texas with them, I figured it was a good stepping stone. It was a way to get away from New Orleans and all the expectations people had of me. A way to get away from my parents..." She looked at him. "Don't get me wrong—my mom and dad are amazing. But my family is...intense. My dad is driven by a need for success, and he expects all his kids to have the same drive. And look at us—we're all at the top of our professions."

"I still don't get why that means you can't open a dress shop."

"For one thing, it will be more than a dress shop." Jack heard that Fortune drive in her voice that she'd just been complaining about. "But to my immediate family, a retail shop...well, it isn't what we do."

He frowned. He hadn't gotten the impression that Beau or Draper were snobs about their name or their business, but he hadn't spent that much time with them. But his brother-in-law, Brady, was a Fortune, and he definitely wasn't that way.

"Did they actually tell you that?"

"Not in those exact words. But they tease me about my shopping…"

"Hey, I've witnessed your shopping skills twice now, and they're nothing to laugh about. You have mad skills at finding what people need." Belle's cheeks went pink and she straightened a little in the seat. Jack felt a stab of anger that her own family hadn't made her feel proud of her unique talents. He kept going, "You can work with any budget—you proved that today. And your sense of color and decorating…I like all the paint colors you made me buy yesterday."

Laughter bubbled up and her eyes brightened. "*Made* you buy? That makes me sound—"

"Like a woman who knows her mind and trusts her instincts? Yes." Belle's mouth had been open to speak, but it snapped shut now in surprise. "I'm just sayin' you have a gift for this stuff, and if that's what you want to do, then you should do it. Go open your boutique and do what you do best."

"Wow." She blinked a few times. "I should have recorded that to play as my daily mantra. You'd make a great motivational speaker."

He chuckled. "Maybe, but it's not what I want to do. You, on the other hand, actually *want* to do something that uses your best talents. Why wait? And don't tell me it's because of your family. You're a grown-ass woman."

She stared as if he'd said something brilliant or shocking. He replayed his words in his head, but they didn't seem all that special to him. Her fingers twisted together in her lap in an uncharacteristic show of uncertainty. He reached over and set his hand over them. Was she trembling? Were those tears shimmering in her eyes? *Damn*.

"What did I say wrong?"

"Nothing," she whispered. She cleared her throat and patted the top of his hand. "You didn't say anything wrong at all."

Belle's back was aching. Every evening that week she'd painted and stripped wallpaper at Jack's place. Every day she ran around the office to make sure everything was on schedule. She also got up early most mornings to review her business plan for Belle's Boutique and scroll through commercial real estate listings in the area. She groaned as she pushed open the door to the local townie bar. She was exhausted. And it was all Jack's fault.

Not the work at the house—she did that happily, glad to spend time with him and see the house shed its 1980s vibe. And running her brothers' office was her job. But the boutique? That was a dream that Jack actually believed in. And that helped her believe in it, too. He was right. What was she waiting for?

It was also Jack's fault that she hadn't had more sleep this week. Ever since their excursion to Austin and his motivational speech, she hadn't been able to get him out of her head. The way her skin sizzled when he was around. The way he did sweet things that didn't mirror his solemn composure. He'd adopted a three-legged dog and managed to toss a new dog bed and fancy bowls for Sarge into their carts at the big-box store. Not only that, but he'd bought toys and a soccer ball to have at the house for his twin nephews. And he bought a pair of leather work gloves for a coworker named Marcus, an older fellow veteran who'd helped Jack learn the unspoken rules of the job at Fortune Brothers Construction.

Were any of these *big* things? Maybe not. But they were evidence of a kind and caring heart inside a man who didn't want anyone else to notice. His sister insisted Jack never smiled, but Belle knew better. He smiled at her. Whether he was chuckling at her splattering paint all over herself when they tackled the great room, or giving her that sexy, slow sideways grin that said… Well, she wasn't sure what it said, but it always made her pulse heat up.

"Belle!" Meg called her name from the bar,

and she waved back. Tonight was supposed to be a girls' night out, so she needed to stop thinking about some man. Except…the man she'd been thinking about was standing right next to her friend. Jack held up his drink in greeting as Belle approached, mouthing "wine?" to her. She nodded, watching Jack lean across the bar to order.

That little moment—him knowing what she'd want and ordering it for her—was surprisingly intimate. Did they have a secret language now? Wasn't that something only romantic couples did? They'd stuck to their agreement to stay away from kissing, but even without that physical connection, their relationship had deepened. And she liked it. She liked *him*. Oh, God.

She was falling for the wrong guy. She was falling for Jack Radcliffe.

He handed her the wineglass with a quizzical smile. "Cabernet, right? You okay? You look like you've seen a ghost."

"I'm fine!" Oh, no—she was doing that nervous shouty thing again. That thing she only did when she was anxious. When she was attracted to someone. She took a breath and held on to it for a moment before letting it go. "I mean, thank you for the wine. It's been a long week."

"And I've been working you too hard."

"That's been fun work." *And I'd like to have fun*

with you right now. She bit the inside of her cheek to punish her misbehaving mind.

"Are you sure you're okay?" he asked, "I didn't mean to crash your night with Meg and the girls." They both looked over to see Meg and her other two triplet sisters laughing together, seemingly oblivious to the two of them. "I promise I'm heading home as soon as I finish my beer."

Please don't...

"Uh-oh." Jack's voice went flat. "Looks like I have a job to do." He put his arm around her shoulder and tugged her close. *What the...?*

She followed his gaze and saw Stefan Mendoza standing in the doorway. He looked around as if searching for someone. Belle felt...nothing. She felt absolutely nothing. Fate or not, Stefan wasn't the man she wanted tonight. She turned to face Jack, resting her hand over his heart.

"Careful, Belle." His voice had a rough edge to it now. "Don't oversell it or Stefan will think he doesn't stand a chance."

Her hand flattened against him, and his eyes darkened. *Go big or go home, Belle.*

"He doesn't," she whispered. "He doesn't stand a chance."

Jack's forehead creased in confusion. "What? I thought the game was to get him to sweep you off your feet."

"I'm not playing games anymore. There's only one man here I want to go home with."

He sucked a deep breath through clenched teeth. "Belle…"

"I mean it, Jack." She laid it all on the line. "Take me home."

"What about Mendoza?"

"What about him?" She reached her free hand up to cup Jack's cheek. "I don't want to talk about anyone but you. And me."

She thought he was going to ask another question. Instead he dipped his head and kissed her. It was soft. Warm. Inviting. Full of promise. She returned it, trying to make it clear with her lips that she meant what she'd said. His arm slid around her waist, his large hand flattening against her back, under her shirt and against her skin. That much skin contact felt like he'd lit a match inside of her. She moaned and pressed against him, standing on her toes.

When his head came up, he searched her face before his mouth slid into that delicious slanted grin. "I'm not asking any more questions. So if you're not sure…"

"Take me home with you, Jack. You're the man I want."

The flecks of gold in his eyes looked like fireworks against the deep brown. His smile wasn't a *half* anything anymore. It was wide, complete and sincere. It made her insides melt into a puddle of feelings. Desire. Anticipation. Confidence. She knew she was making the right choice. But there were other mysterious feelings floating around in that puddle. Feelings she couldn't define and didn't dare examine.

It was Meg's voice that broke the spell. "Something tells me you're not finishing that wine, cousin. Mind if I take it?"

Ashley snorted. "I don't think either one of them heard you."

"Get a room, you two!" Nicole chuckled.

Jack started to laugh, his eyes staying fixed on Belle as he answered her cousin. "Take the wine. Take the beer." He slapped a twenty on the counter behind Belle. "I'm taking Belle home."

Meg grinned. "And is Belle on board with that?"

Their eyes were still locked tight when Belle answered. "Very."

How they made it the short distance to Jack's house without him driving his truck straight into a ditch was beyond Belle. They couldn't keep their hands off each other. Now that they'd given themselves permission to touch, to kiss, to follow their desires wherever they led, the cab of the truck was turning into a red-hot love scene. Her hands slid up between his legs as he drove. He turned and kissed her hard, slanting his eyes toward the road as his tongue slid into her mouth. His hand entwined in her hair, pulling her head back for better access. *Yes, please.*

The truck finally came to a stop. She looked up at the shadow of his house, still unsure how he'd managed to find the right place. He unclipped his seat belt and was on her in a flash, reaching over to recline the seat. He freed her seat belt as he kissed her deep and hard, his hands racing up and down her sides, sliding under her top to finally cup her breasts. She arched her back with a whimper, wanting more. She must have said the word out loud, because he laughed against the skin at the base of her neck.

"I'll give you more. I'll give you everything. But not here in the driveway. Come on."

He led her into the house. She was clutching his hand so tightly she was surprised he wasn't protesting. She'd only had one sip of wine, so that wasn't what made her stagger. She was drunk on her need.

Sarge bounded out of his crate to greet them. Jack told Belle that Sarge was reliable in the house, so he'd stopped locking the crate door. After so many long months at the shelter, the dog seemed to find security in the confines of the crate and went in there on his own. Sarge took a few laps

**Claim up to FOUR NEW BOOKS & TWO MYSTERY GIFTS –
absolutely FREE!**

Dear Reader,

We both know life can be difficult at times. That's why it's important to treat yourself so you can relax and recharge once in a while.

And I'd like to help you do this by sending you this amazing offer of up to FOUR brand new full length FREE BOOKS that WE pay for.

This is everything I have ready to send to you right now:

Try **Harlequin® Special Edition** books featuring comfort and strength in the support of loved ones and enjoying the journey no matter what life throws your way.

Try **Harlequin® Heartwarming™ Larger-Print** books featuring uplifting stories where the bonds of friendship, family and community unite.

Or **TRY BOTH!**

All we ask in return is that you answer 4 simple questions on the attached Treat Yourself survey. You'll get **Two Free Books** and **Two Mystery Gifts** from each series you try, *altogether worth over $20*! Who could pass up a deal like that?

Sincerely,

Pam Powers

Harlequin Reader Service

Treat Yourself to Free Books and Free Gifts.

Answer 4 fun questions and get rewarded.

We love to connect with our readers! Please tell us a little about you...

	YES	NO
1. I LOVE reading a good book.	○	○
2. I indulge and "treat" myself often.	○	○
3. I love getting FREE things.	○	○
4. Reading is one of my favorite activities.	○	○

TREAT YOURSELF • Pick your 2 Free Books...

Yes! Please send me my Free Books from each series I select and Free Mystery Gifts. I understand that I am under no obligation to buy anything, as explained on the back of this card.

Which do you prefer?

❏ **Harlequin® Special Edition** 235/335 HDL GRCC
❏ **Harlequin® Heartwarming™ Larger-Print** 161/361 HDL GRCC
❏ **Try Both** 235/335 & 161/361 HDL GRCN

FIRST NAME	LAST NAME

ADDRESS

APT.#	CITY

STATE/PROV.	ZIP/POSTAL CODE

EMAIL ❏ Please check this box if you would like to receive newsletters and promotional emails from Harlequin Enterprises ULC and its affiliates. You can unsubscribe anytime.

SE/HW-820-TY22

around the backyard while Jack took a few laps around Belle's mouth with his tongue, leaving her more breathless than the dog was.

The furniture had arrived a few days ago and the painting was done. The bedroom was still a little bare, with no art or rugs or drapes. But the warm gray walls looked good with the dark floors and heavy arts and crafts furniture. Belle looked around and smiled. It was perfect for Jack. Simple. Clean. Functional. No frills.

He surprised her by wrapping his arm around her waist and lifting her up. She squealed and giggled as he swung her into his arms and dropped her onto the bed, crawling across the mattress after her as she scrambled toward the headboard.

Then Jack swore. Sarge had joined them on the bed, eager to play whatever game his humans were playing. Jack put him on the floor and told him to scram, but Sarge stayed right next to the bed, watching their every move.

"Dude," Jack muttered. "You're killing the mood!" Jack stood and tried getting the dog out of the bedroom. That quickly became a fun new game. Sarge bolted around him every time he tried to close the door. Jack put his hands on his hips and scowled. Belle got off the bed and, between the two of them and a few bacon treats, they managed to distract the dog in the kitchen long enough for them to run full speed for the bedroom and close the door. Sarge barked once and snuffled around the door for a minute before he got bored and wandered off.

Jack fell onto the bed, covering his face with his arm. Belle lay next to him and soaked in the sound of him laughing so hard he was wheezing. She reached out for his hand, whispering his name. Jack's laughter faded, and he rose up on his knees, staring down at her. She slid toward the head of the bed again, and he grabbed her ankle with a playful grin. How her clothes weren't bursting into flames under the heat in his eyes was a mystery. She could feel burning inside her chest, and something was boiling in her abdomen. It felt like lava—heavy molten desire pinning her to the mattress, her back against the headboard.

Jack's hands traced their way slowly up her legs, from ankles to calves to the surprisingly sensitive skin behind her knees. His lips followed his right hand, leaving a trail of light kisses. She felt every place he kissed her, even after he'd moved on. As if he'd left his stamp on her, hot and bright. He pushed her skirt higher, and she watched. Because watching him at work was mesmerizing.

Just as she prepared for him to reach the smoldering fire between her thighs, he pushed himself up on his arms and moved higher. As he leaned down to kiss her lips, it was as if he'd changed gears again. Slower. Less hurried. Less teasing. Determined.

She kissed him back, wrapping her arms tightly around his neck, pressing her hips up against the ridge she felt in his jeans. He wanted to be sure she was along for this ride, and oh, yes, she definitely was. She slid her tongue into his mouth and felt his whole body shudder.

"Belle…"

He didn't even need to ask.

"Yes. Please, Jack." She nipped at the edge of his chin. "Make love to me."

Chapter Eight

Jack was dreaming. It was the only explanation for Belle Fortune wrapped around him, literally begging him for sex. He was glad to hear her put her wants into words so there was no confusion about what they both wanted. Although it hardly took a genius to know they wanted the same thing. And his body was absolutely burning for release. But this was Belle. She deserved more than some wham-bam-thank-you-ma'am.

"We have a problem," Belle said, her voice full of concern.

Oh, no. Had he spent so much time lost in his own head that she'd changed her mind?

"What is it?"

"We still have clothes on."

Her eyes sparkled and he couldn't help it. He laughed again. Partly from relief and partly because the moment was so *them*. Honest with a dose of snark. As he laughed, he realized that he hadn't laughed—really laughed—in a very long time. Now he'd done it twice in the span of a few minutes with her. Even his lungs seemed surprised. He could almost feel them happily expanding in his chest to pull in more air.

Belle looked up at him with wide eyes.

"You definitely need to do that more often."

"Do what?"

"Laugh. You have a great laugh." Her smile turned mischievous. "But you can laugh later. Right now, we still have too many clothes on, Jack."

"That's easy enough to fix."

He was still straddling her, so he straightened on his knees and yanked his shirt over his head. She sat up and did the same, revealing a lacy blue bra that matched her eyes. It was cute but it needed to go. She reached behind her back in silent agreement. The move brought her face closer to his body, which was tight with anticipation. He reached down and cupped the back of her head, brushing his fingers through her silky hair. She looked up at him through her golden eyelashes as her breasts fell free. Then she looked at the belt buckle in front of her face and reached for it.

Now Jack *knew* he was dreaming. He didn't move. Couldn't move. He bit out a curse and pushed her back on the mattress. It took him a moment to find the side zipper on her skirt, but he managed to get it off without ripping it apart. He was hungry enough for her that he would have torn it from her body if he had to. Especially when he saw that heat in her eyes that practically dared him to do just that. Her panties slid down with the skirt. All the way down her legs and over the sky-high heels she had on.

"The shoes can stay." He held up her foot, kissing the top of it. He shed his own clothes and lowered himself over her. He wanted to appreciate every instant of this night. Take it slow. Make it memorable. But God, he wanted her. Right now. He kissed her until she was moaning and wriggling beneath him. Every time she lifted against his hardness, it sent shock waves through his body. He ground his teeth together and ordered himself to go slow. He had to go slow.

"Now, Jack. Now!" Belle's voice broke.

He grabbed at the nightstand for a condom, tearing into the foil package with his teeth and rolling it on as quickly as possible. Screw waiting. He settled into her slowly, not wanting to hurt her. But this was Belle Fortune, and she was a take-charge woman. She lifted her hips and took him in with a hiss, her eyes falling closed. His jaw clenched and he counted to ten in his head, trying to wrestle some sort of control back from her. He finally began to move again.

Belle let out a long soft sigh and surrendered, following his lead. And it was… It was more than just sex. For the first time, Jack thought he knew what making love felt like. Every move was in perfect synchronization. Every breath. Every heartbeat. He didn't know where he ended and she began. Was it corny to think they'd become one?

They didn't need words. They understood each other's every moan and move. When the pace picked up, he had no idea who'd started it. They breathed each other's names. Then they shouted them out loud. After that, nothing made sense and everything made sense. The intensity went wild, and finally he couldn't hold on to his control any longer. He exploded with a drawn-out groan and she followed with a little gasp. Her nails dug into his back, then her arms slid into a hug. More like the clasp of a drowning person trying to stay afloat.

He knew exactly how she felt.

* * *

When Jack moved off her to dispose of the condom, Belle put her hand over her heart. Just to make sure it was still there. Still beating. Because she was pretty certain she'd just died. And it had been awesome.

On some level, she'd wanted this ever since the night they kissed at the office open house. That was when he'd lit the fuse. Ever since that frantic kiss on her brother's desk, she'd wanted to sleep with Jack Radcliffe. She simply hadn't admitted it to herself—or to him—until tonight.

And then he'd laughed. *Really* laughed. And she'd fallen head over heels. It wasn't about the physical attraction. It was about the man.

The mattress sank as Jack rejoined her in bed. She turned her head and took in the sight of him. Long, lean and hard. A few scars here and there— from childhood or from combat? A tattoo she hadn't seen before—a Celtic band around his right bicep, with an odd-shaped opening in the center and two crossed swords inside.

"What's that?" She reached up and touched the tattoo. He didn't even glance at it.

"Tattoo."

She rolled her eyes. "No kidding. What does it mean?"

"It means I got drunk one night and woke up

with a sore arm." He stretched out next to her. "Is that really what you want to talk about right now?"

"I feel bad that I never noticed it. What do the swords mean?"

He sighed and draped his arm around her waist, pulling her back against his chest so she couldn't see his face, which he buried against the base of her neck.

"Not swords. Bayonets." His voice was muffled by her skin.

"What's the difference?"

He didn't answer right away.

"You smell really good." He kissed her softly, sending shivers down her spine. She snuggled against him, getting the message. He didn't want to talk, and she wasn't about to ruin the moment by pestering him. She couldn't help wanting to know more about him. Or, more precisely, everything about him. But they had time. And his fingers had just found her breasts, destroying her concentration.

They made love again, but spent more time getting there. Kissing. Exploring. Whispering. Coming together and staying together for a long, methodic buildup to the escape they couldn't hold off any longer. They fell asleep in a sex-exhausted tangle of sheets, arms and legs.

The room was dark when Belle opened her eyes

again. She was alone. The bathroom was dark, too, but there was a light coming from the hall, and she could smell something cooking. The minute the scent invaded her nostrils, she realized how hungry she was. She scrambled out of bed, pulling on her skirt and top. She stopped in the bathroom to freshen up and pull her hair back into a low ponytail. She looked pretty basic, but it wasn't like he hadn't already seen everything.

Jack was standing at the stove in well-worn fleece pants that had been cut into shorts. And nothing else. His hair was standing on end. Sarge came to greet her, bringing her presence to Jack's attention.

He smiled, and it came more easily than it usually did. "Hey. I was going to wake you when the food was ready." He waved a spatula toward her. "What we did tonight was definitely worth skipping dinner for, but I woke up starving."

"As soon as I smelled food, so was I. Whatcha' cookin'?" She walked over to where he was sprinkling shredded cheddar cheese into a skillet.

"Cheese omelet and breakfast sausages."

"Breakfast for dinner?"

He pointed to the clock on the stovetop.

"Breakfast for breakfast. It's morning."

And technically, he was right. It was thirty minutes past midnight. She pulled two dishes from the cupboard and put them on the counter near the stove.

"A man who can cook. Very impressive."

He folded the omelet over the melting cheese and divided it between the two plates. He looked over his shoulder as he turned toward the microwave.

"First, I'd prefer if you were impressed by what happened in my bedroom—"

"Oh, I was."

"And second…" He showed her the plate of precooked frozen sausage links he pulled from the microwave. "Don't get *too* excited. I can grill. I can make pasta sauce. I can make omelets. And I can pop things into the microwave."

They sat at the kitchen table together. Sarge hopped over and curled up at Belle's feet. She took a bite of her omelet and groaned.

"This is *so* good." She grinned down at Sarge. "I guess he approves of you having company."

He grunted. "He approves of anyone with food."

It was odd how normal this felt. Her with Jack. "So who taught you how to cook pasta sauce and omelets?"

"My mom. She knew my attention span in the kitchen was short, so she taught me a few dishes that were either quick, like omelets, or that could make multiple meals, like a big pot of pasta sauce."

He was already taking the last bite of his omelet, stacked on his fork with the last of his sausage. Then he looked down at Sarge and pulled a piece of sausage off his fork and tossed it to the dog, who caught it in midair. "This dog is wacky."

Belle laughed. "Because he likes sausage? News flash—all dogs do."

"I know that. But the way he was determined to be with us in the bedroom cracked me up. There's only one mystery…" He shook his finger playfully at the dog. "He keeps losing tennis balls. I've bought him a dozen of those things, and they keep vanishing. I don't know if he's burying them or what."

"Either that or eating them."

Jack chuckled. "I doubt that. He's fed very well." She stared at Jack until he finally asked. "What?"

"Look at us! We're sitting here half-dressed eating a midnight meal like we've been out clubbing. We're talking about your dog. After we made love that was… It was…"

"Orgasmic?"

"I think that's a given." She winked. "It's just…"

"What comes next?"

"Yeah. What comes next?"

She stood, taking their plates and setting them in the sink. He followed her and wrapped his arms around her waist when she turned. He tugged lightly on her hair until she was looking up at him, her chin resting on his chest.

"First up is a decision. Do you want to go back to the hotel, or do you want to spend the night?"

"Definitely the latter."

"Good. What comes next is me making love to you again. And maybe again after that. Maybe we'll squeeze a little sleep in there before sunrise." He lifted one shoulder. "Maybe."

"That sounds like an excellent plan. But, Jack—"

"But nothing. We'll talk in the daylight, when we're clearheaded and fully clothed." He put his hands on her shoulders and turned her, smacking her bottom lightly to send her out of the kitchen. "I'll tell you this much…I don't want this to be our only night."

Belle smiled as she walked ahead of him to the bedroom. That sounded like another good plan. She wanted more nights like this, too.

The sky outside the glass doors to the bedroom's private veranda was beginning to turn pinkish-gray. Jack leaned back against the headboard and watched as it slowly brightened. Daylight was coming. But right now, the room was still dark and warm. And Belle Fortune was snuggled against him, her head on his chest, her fingers tracing random circles on his skin.

Her golden hair was wild, spread across her shoulders and tumbling onto his chest. Her breathing was synced with his. Their heartbeats, too. It didn't make sense, the way they fit together. The way she felt like a completion of him. He kissed the top of her head and she made a purring sound of contentment.

"What time do you need to be at work?"

She buried her face against him with a groan. "Work schmerk. They can live without me for a day. Let's stay here."

"I don't have the luxury of working for family. I have to go to work, so you may as well, too."

She lifted her head and looked around the dark room.

"It's still nighttime."

"Not for long."

Her arms tightened around him, her voice pouty. "I don't want to get up."

"We have a little time yet." He stroked her shoulder. "Why don't you try to get some sleep."

Lord knew they hadn't had much sleep last night. Maybe a few naps in between making love, then snuggling themselves into knots like they were now. Like their bodies couldn't get enough of each other. He tugged the sheet up over her and kissed her head again. Who knew he could be the kind of guy to ever enjoy the cuddling as much as he'd enjoyed the sex?

"I'm not sleepy." She looked up at him with a lopsided grin, her lips still kiss-swollen. "I'm exhausted, but I'm not sleepy. I feel like my whole body is just…humming, you know?"

"Yeah, I know. Me, too."

She ran her finger along the tattoo on his bicep. "You never did tell me about the difference between swords and bayonets."

It must have been the exhaustion that made him more willing to go there. Or maybe it was this woman in his arms who'd charmed him enough to open that door.

"Bayonets are like a dagger. They're beveled, and they can be clipped onto a rifle barrel."

"And what's this they're inside of?"

"It's a keg of gunpowder. It's the badge of the 10th Mountain Division at Fort Drum in upstate New York."

"That was your division? Did you live at Fort Drum?"

"When I wasn't deployed."

"Was it cold there?"

Her questions were curious, not pushy.

"It was hella cold there in the winter. And hot in the summer. Spring is black fly season, which is the worst season there. It was pretty in the fall, though." He shifted his weight, pulling her onto his lap. "But not as pretty as you."

Belle rolled her eyes. "I've got bedhead. And I didn't take my makeup off so I probably look like a clown. But thanks for saying it anyway."

He cupped her face in his hands. "I have *never* seen anything as beautiful as you right this instant. You look…uninhibited. And very, very satisfied."

She laughed, smacking his shoulder. Right where he'd torn the muscle months ago. "Now you're just fishing for compliments! You know I'm satisfied." Her smile faded. "I hit the bad shoulder again, didn't I? Sorry." She leaned forward and kissed it. "How'd you hurt it?"

"I…uh…fell on it." That wasn't a lie. "Wrenched it pretty good."

"Did you see a lot of combat?"

He didn't answer right away. She kissed his shoulder again, then kissed his lips with a soft smile.

"Let me guess…you don't want to talk about it. That's okay. I can wait."

He stayed silent. He didn't want to mislead her that he'd ever want to discuss his combat experiences. He didn't want to hurt her feelings about it either. So he returned the kiss, laying her back onto the mattress. He'd deal with the other stuff later.

* * *

He barely made it to the job site on time. Naturally, it had to be a day when Callum Fortune decided to pay a visit. Jack checked his watch. Technically he had five minutes to spare, but he was usually on-site a good half hour before the crew got started.

Thankfully, Marcus Lawler was there, showing Callum the progress they'd made on the large home being framed out in the new housing tract. Marcus was in his early sixties, his short salt-and-pepper beard stark against his dark skin. He and Jack were coleaders of the crew on this build site. Callum and Marcus made it clear that Jack needed to prove himself before he'd have a work crew of his own. He got it. But he was kicking himself for being late.

It had been really hard to leave his bed—more specifically, leave Belle—that morning. They'd welcomed the dawn making love. Then she'd joined him in the shower and that was another delay. Then he'd had to drop her at the hotel for the walk of shame in the same outfit she'd worn last night.

"G'morning, Callum. Marcus. I…uh…lost track of time. Sorry—won't happen again."

"Easy, Jack," Callum said with a laugh. "You're still on time. And the project is looking good." He squinted and tipped his head before pointing at Jack's neck. "Marcus, I think I've found the reason why Jack lost track of time this morning."

Marcus leaned in and his eyes went wide. "By gosh, I think you're right. That's definitely lipstick, and it's not Jack's shade."

Jack closed his eyes and slapped his hand to his neck. Belle had kissed him goodbye at the hotel. More than once. He never thought about her lipstick leaving evidence behind. Both men were laughing, so there was no sense denying it.

"Yeah, yeah, okay. I had a good night and a better morning. That's no excuse to run late."

Callum winked before turning away. "I don't know. I've had the same…um…problem some mornings, and that little bit of time right before the day gets started is always worth it. Anyone we know?"

Jack coughed and cleared his throat. He didn't want to lie. But he damn sure didn't want to tell Callum he'd spent last night with his young cousin. Callum's smile faded.

"Oh, so my wife and sister were right with all their gossip. You and cousin Belle?"

Jack straightened, his shoulders tight. "I don't feel right talking about Belle when she's not here. As far as what we did or didn't do…"

Callum put his hand up to stop him. "Please,

God, do *not* tell me what you two did or didn't do. I was out of line to ask and don't need details. It's not me you need to be worried about as much as her brothers. The New Orleans Fortunes are a tight unit, and she's the baby of the family." Callum changed the subject back to the house, and pointed out a few minor issues he wanted changed.

The new tract was part of Fortune Brothers Construction's promise to Rambling Rose, made back when they built the Hotel Fortune. Their original plan was for a much larger hotel, and the locals were not happy. A compromise had been reached with a more boutique-sized hotel and a promise to hire locals and improve existing businesses. When Kane Fortune joined the company, he'd suggested that better housing options be part of that community promise.

Marcus gave Jack the side-eye all day, but it wasn't until they were packing up that he finally brought up what he'd clearly been dying to talk about.

"Takes some guts to date the boss's cousin, man. The whole town of Rambling Rose is one big Fortune family reunion." He shook his head. "I get that it's tough *not* to date a Fortune when they're everywhere, but that's a lot of eyeballs on you."

Jack tossed his leather toolbelt in the back of the truck. "It just sort of happened. Besides, I don't think of her as being 'a Fortune.'" He made air quotes with his fingers. "I think of her as Belle."

The woman who'd turned his world upside down and inside out last night. The woman who'd texted him an hour ago to say she'd be at his place tonight with an overnight bag. When she made up her mind what she wanted, she took it. And now she'd taken him.

"Have you told her about your nightmares?"

The question came out of nowhere, and Jack stepped back with a frown. He'd told Marcus about that in confidence. True, the older man wasn't breaking it, but he hadn't expected to have it thrown back at him.

Marcus had served in the Middle East. He'd been involved in the kind of conflicts that didn't get fancy titles, but were every bit as dangerous. Jack knew it before Marcus even mentioned it— he'd recognized the sometimes tense composure, the serious approach to problems, the lack of casual chitchat. He recognized himself. One night after work, Marcus had handed Jack a soda from his cooler and asked when and where he'd served. He'd apologized for it not being a beer, explaining he'd been sober for five years.

They'd talked awhile, the way only two soldiers could—in half sentences and vague code for the things they saw in battle. No need for messy details. War was war. Same job, different setting. *Felt like stateside* meant the deployment was easy. Boring. *It was a little hairy* meant it was bad—worse than any civilian would understand. *It got bad* meant it was horrible. Bloody. Deadly. The type of event that would haunt people's nightmares. The way one haunted Jack's.

And somehow he'd let that slip to Marcus. Waking up in night sweats. Unwilling to let himself go to sleep after for fear of what he might see. Marcus told Jack he should talk to someone. But they were just dreams. Dreams disturbed your sleep. That was it.

"I'm good, Marcus. No nightmares with Belle. Maybe they're gone now."

Marcus studied him for a moment, then shrugged. "Maybe. Be careful, though. Women wanna know stuff. Stuff you won't want to talk about."

"I already made it clear I don't want to talk about my military time. She understands."

Marcus turned and walked away to his beat-up truck, fresh out of the shop. He'd told Jack he lived alone and liked it that way. His wife had left him back when he was drinking, taking their two sons and daughter with her. He was working on rebuilding relationships with his kids, but said he was better off by himself. Too jaded for any woman to put up with. Marcus opened the door to the truck and

turned back to Jack. His expression was somewhere between amused and worried. His mouth
was smiling. His eyes? Not so much.

"She understands, huh? Lucky you. Don't say
I didn't warn you."

Chapter Nine

Belle was struggling to keep her eyes open as she rifled through the file cabinets in the office, making sure everything was in order. She knew it was, since *she* was the one who filed everything, and she was meticulous. Of course, all their client information was in digital form, too, but Dad was old-school. He wanted paper records as backup in case of some nameless online threat, like a hacker somehow holding their cloud data hostage.

She had to do something that required standing so she wouldn't nod off at her desk. Staying at Jack's house for the past four nights had been wonderful—she'd basically moved in. Maybe that was too fast, but it was a matter of practicality, too. Why drive back to Hotel Fortune in the middle of the night when she could stay snuggled in his arms? And she was so tired of living at the hotel, no matter how nice it was.

Jack's house was spacious—if mostly empty—and the veranda was perfect for dining during this warm stretch. She and Jack would watch the sunsets, wineglasses in hand, while Sarge went on the hunt for a squirrel to chase. It was perfect. Except for the lack of sleep.

It wasn't just all the nighttime activity that kept her awake, though that was fun—like fireworks-on-the-Fourth-of-July kind of fun. But Jack was so restless in his sleep, and it worried Belle enough to keep her awake. They'd fall asleep wrapped up together, but a few hours later he'd be twitching all over, flinching as if he was being struck, mumbling in his sleep. And then he'd go dead still, and that was when she worried the most. It wasn't relaxation. His whole body went tight, as if he was frozen.

Belle would stroke him and whisper that he was safe, and usually he'd let out a long breath and go back to sleep. Sometimes he'd clutch her so close that she could barely breathe, and she'd hug him right back, letting him know she was there for him.

In the morning, he'd swear he didn't remember dreaming. He'd apologize and tell her he was fine, and that she must be a light sleeper. It was true she hadn't lived with a guy in a long time—not since her senior year in college. But she knew distress when she saw it. Still, if he didn't want to talk about it, she wouldn't push him.

But last night had been different. They were both sound asleep when Jack suddenly cried out a man's name. *Jimmy!* And again, even louder, sounding terrified. His entire body began to shake.

"No...no..." His head thrashed back and forth. "Where's our air cover? Oh, God..." He was in a cold sweat by then, and Belle had whispered his name, trying to wake him as gently as possible. Her heart was breaking for him. Then he'd yelled something she couldn't understand and sat upright, his eyes open but unfocused. Belle sat up next to him and touched his shoulder. He'd reacted as if she'd hit him with a stun gun, spinning around, looking as if he didn't even know who she was.

He'd blinked, then scrubbed his hands over his face. "Sorry. Damn." He looked at her. "Did I hurt you?"

"No, not at all." She put her arms around him and he held on to her like she was a lifeline. "But you scared me. Jack, where are these dreams coming from? Is it...is it PTSD?"

"No." His voice was firm. "Nothing like that.

Just a bad dream. I'm sorry, babe." He kissed her, but she could tell he was distracted.

"Tell me what happened in your dream." She could help him if she understood.

Jack's whole demeanor had changed. His body tensed up again and his voice turned hard. "I don't remember. Let's get back to sleep. G'night." A quick kiss and he'd turned over and went to sleep. Or at least pretended to. She had a feeling he'd lain awake the rest of the night, just as she had.

"Is there a spider on the wall or something?" Her brother Draper's voice startled her so much that Belle dropped the folder she was holding. Papers went sailing across the floor. Draper took her arm. "Hey, are you okay? Where were you?"

She brushed his hand away and started scooping up the papers, her face burning. "Sorry. I didn't hear you come in. I'm tired. I guess I zoned out."

"Wouldn't have anything to do with that construction worker you're madly in love with, would it?"

She looked up from where she'd crouched on the floor. "What does *that* mean?"

Draper grabbed the rest of the papers and put them on the desk. "Come on. You're in love with love, sis. I like that you're such a starry-eyed romantic, but I don't want to see you get hurt."

Belle stood, slapping the folder down on the

desk. She was exhausted, so her usually long fuse when it came to her family was extremely short today. She waved her finger in his face and he stepped back in surprise.

"That's rich, coming from the family playboy. Back home you had a different woman on your arm every time I saw you, Draper Fortune, and I'm sure the same will be true in Texas." Belle had a feeling Draper considered beautiful women to be accessories, like his fancy cars and fine wines.

He threw his hands up with a laugh. "Hey, I never claimed to fall in love with any of them!"

"Whatever," Belle growled. "You don't know *anything* about my love life. You're remembering me when I was a teenager with pictures of boy bands in my bedroom. I'm all grown up, damn it! Even if no one in my family wants to admit it." She did everything but stomp her feet. Draper almost laughed again, then seemed to think better of it.

"You're right. It's just…you're our little Tinkerbelle, and—"

"Puh-leez stop calling me that." Belle's teeth ground together.

"Okay, okay." He held up his hands. "I get it. You're grown-up. But you'll always be my baby sister. You know I love you, right?"

Her anger deflated as fast as it had risen. "I know. But if everyone keeps seeing me as a cute little Tinkerbelle with stars in her eyes, I feel like I'll be stuck in Neverland forever. I'm a grown woman. I'm in a relationship—a very new relationship—with a grown man. A man who's been to war and seen things." She could only imagine what, since he refused to talk about it. "We're still learning about each other. It's a lot. And being laughed at doesn't help."

Draper frowned. "What do you mean when you say *it's a lot*. If that guy's not treating you right…"

"If he wasn't treating me right, I wouldn't be with him. This is what an actual relationship looks like, Draper. It's work sometimes."

"I thought the whole point of a real relationship was that it *wasn't* work. And who's laughing at you?"

Belle moved to the desk Draper was leaning against and started putting the papers in order. Sometimes she thought her two youngest brothers were clueless when it came to romance. Then again, she'd thought that about all her brothers at one point or another. She shook her head.

"You don't think Mom and Dad have to work at their relationship?" she asked. "And they're more in love than anyone I know. Mom always says, 'Anything worth anything is worth working for.'" She looked up. "And *you* laugh at me. Every chance you get."

"I thought Mom was talking about business when she said that." He straightened, putting his hands on her shoulders and turning her to face him. "And I don't ever want you thinking I'm laughing at you to be cruel. It's…it's affectionate laughter. Like I'd laugh at…" His voice trailed off as he realized he was digging a hole.

"Like you'd laugh at a cute little kid?" She stepped back. "Let me ask you something, Draper. Would you laugh at your office manager like that if it was anyone other than me?"

His mouth fell open. "Well…no…but…"

She crossed her arms and arched a brow at him. She didn't need to speak. Just wait.

"Belle…I…uh…" His mouth snapped shut and remorse filled his face. "Damn. I didn't see it that way." His eyes closed. "Which makes me an even bigger jerk." A new knowledge dawned in his eyes. "I've got this weird slideshow running in my head right now of things I've teased you about. Why didn't you kick my ass a long time ago?"

Again, she didn't need to answer. He was clearly working it out on his own. His cheeks reddened a little.

"I'll do better, I promise." He nodded at her. "And I'll make sure Beau does, too. You're a big part of why we've gotten off to such a great start in Rambling Rose, Belle. And now I'll take off my coworker hat and be your brother." He leaned over to look straight into her eyes. "Are you happy here?"

"Yeah. Sure."

"And you're happy with this Radcliffe guy?"

She smiled without needing to think about it.

"Very."

His forehead wrinkled, but he didn't say anything right away. Finally he pulled her in for a quick hug.

"Before you ask—no, I wouldn't do this with any office manager but you. Or this…" He held her out at arm's length. "Take the afternoon off. Go take a nap. Talk to your guy. Go shopping. Maybe not in that order."

Jack had to stop at the veterinary clinic on his way home. Callum told him his sister wanted to add some more shelving in one of the rooms, and asked Jack to get the measurements and figure out what was needed. He didn't mind a little delay in getting home. Not that he didn't want to be with Belle, but he had a feeling she wasn't going to let last night go.

His first thought when he'd woken up in a cold sweat and realized she was there was that he may have hurt her somehow. There were times when his nightmares ripped the sheets from the bed. The idea of putting her at risk made him feel ill. The nightmares had to stop eventually. They had to.

The young woman at the desk told him Stephanie was in back, where the Paws and Claws rescue animals were. The closer he got, the louder the unearthly howls were. He half expected to see a mountain lion when he opened the door. Instead, Stephanie and a teenage girl were holding a scraggly-looking black cat on the examination table. Stephanie had a syringe in her hand, and was cooing to the yowling cat.

"It's all over, pretty girl. You didn't even feel it." The cat stopped, but glowered at her with a low growl that went up and down the musical scale. Stephanie laughed. "Such a drama queen, Diva."

"Which is it?" Jack asked. "Drama queen or diva?" He cautiously approached and reached toward the cat, who stopped growling and tipped her head toward his hand to be petted. "Whoa. That was a change in tune."

Stephanie looked at the girl holding the cat. "Well, I'll be darned. You were right, Kelly. She needs to be a man's cat." She smiled at Jack. "To answer your question, she *is* a drama queen, and her *name* is Diva. Kelly's been trying to tell me Diva hates women, and now I get it. You need another companion?"

"I've got my hands full with the companions I have."

"Plural? So it's true—you and Belle?"

"Uh…yeah." Him and his big mouth. "You needed some shelves built?"

"Nice change of subject."

He turned to follow her, then took one last look at Diva. She had a shiny black coat, but there was a chunk missing from one ear, and her tail had a weird crook to it. There was a scar on one lip that gave her a permanent sneer.

"What's her story?"

Stephanie walked to one corner of the room. "Diva was a stray, so we don't know her story. She's about three years old, and she's been with the rescue for four months now. She's another hard-to-place pet, like Sarge was." She gestured to the alcove where she wanted shelves added. "I think we can fit five fixed shelves in here, about eighteen inches deep."

"Sure," Jack replied. "Why is Diva hard to place? Because of her ear?"

"The ear. The tail. The lip. She looks feral, but she's not a bad cat. She's just seen stuff. And she doesn't like being with other cats or dogs. She really is a diva—she is not into sharing. Probably just as well you don't take her home, since she'd probably beat up poor Sarge. Add in the fact that people prefer kittens to adult cats. And black cats in general are harder to place, which is dumb."

"So you're saying you need to find a single guy with no pets."

"Exactly. One who isn't fussy about her looks, and can put up with her snobbery."

He measured the corner and sketched out what she wanted and didn't mention the cat again. The shelves would be an easy project. He almost forgot about his worries about talking to Belle that night. Until he got home and walked into a transformed house.

The great room now sported a huge rug in sunset colors. There was artwork on the walls. Clearly Belle had been shopping.

He headed down to the bedroom to shower and change, only to find *that* room had been dressed up, too. Curtains. A new rug. Black and white nature photos on one wall. And, interestingly enough, that framed rose painting from Belle's hotel room was on the dresser. She still hadn't figured out where or who it came from or what the strange inscription meant, but she hadn't parted with it. And now it was in his bedroom.

He'd told Marcus he didn't think of Belle as "a Fortune," but in reality, that's what she was. They hadn't talked about money, but he knew she must have a lot of it. He also knew Belle liked to shop. Furnishing *his* home with *her* money was not going to fly with him, though.

After a quick shower, he found Belle outside on the veranda with Sarge. Her back was to him, but he was sure she'd heard him. The table was set, and a pan of lasagna sat in the center. He'd been oddly surprised at what a great cook Belle was. He'd figured the Fortunes had hired help for the cooking, but she'd quickly disabused him of that idea.

Sarge was grinning at him from his spot at Belle's feet. Darn traitor of a dog—he followed the woman around like she was an angel. Belle's hair was loose and she was wearing some wispy, gauzy thing for a dress. Jack could understand Sarge's confusion. The edges of his anger softened, but he and Belle still needed to talk.

His angel apparently had the power to read his mind. She stood and turned, splaying her hands in a show of innocence. "I know it looks like a lot, but this house just didn't feel like a home, Jack. What I did was presumptuous and pushy and it probably looks like I'm making myself way too comfortable…" She paused to give him a chance to deny it. *Not a chance.* The corner of her mouth lifted. "O-kay. So I *did* overstep. But doesn't it look great?"

"That's not the point."

She walked up and took his hands, her eyes bright. "So you like it?"

"The point is I can't have you buying thousands of dollars of stuff for my house. My *rented* house." He gave her a firm look. "I'm not some charity project."

Her face fell at his last sentence.

"Oh, Jack. That's not what I— I'd never— I just thought it would look nice. And trust me, it was nowhere near thousands. It wasn't even *one* thousand. You should know by now that I know how to shop *and* how to negotiate." She smiled. "Come sit and eat, and I'll tell you about it. Your sister put me onto an amazing shop that does estate sales and consignments, and Harper gave me the Ansel Adams prints in the bedroom. I guess Brady had them before they met, and she wasn't crazy about them."

She was talking fast, pleading her case. She pointed at the table and Jack sat down. Belle filled their plates, talking nonstop.

"And yes, I bought a couple of new pictures. And the curtains." She shrugged. "But the rugs needed some art to connect with, and the windows looked naked. I didn't spend a lot, but if you want me to return them I will. But you could also count it as my share of the rent." She froze, her wineglass halfway to her lips. "Not that I'm officially moved in.

We're not roommates or anything official…" Her shoulders fell along with her expression. "What *are* we…officially?"

That was a really good question. He took a bite of the lasagna and closed his eyes. She'd outdone herself again.

"This is delicious. How'd you get all of this done after work?" He gestured at the table and swept his arm toward the house.

"Draper gave me the afternoon off. I wanted to check out the estate sale place, and things sort of took off from there." She shrugged. "Once the re-tail therapy bug kicks in, it's hard for me to stop. Are you mad about it?"

It helped a little that she'd shopped at a second-hand store and not that expensive store he'd seen at The Shoppes at Rambling Rose. And he wasn't surprised his sister was involved. Harper could make a dollar last longer than anyone he knew.

"I *was* mad," he admitted. "I thought you'd burned through all your platinum credit cards on stuff for me, and that's not the kind of guy I am."

"I know." She reached out and took his hand. "When I saw that big southwestern rug, I knew right away it belonged in your great room, and then one thing led to another."

She gave him a sheepish grin. His anger was gone completely now. For one thing, she hadn't spent a ton. For another, she wasn't asking about his nightmare.

"That rug does look good in there," he admitted. "I know *you* didn't carry that thing inside. How'd you get it all delivered so fast?"

"Oh, you'd be surprised what I can charm people into doing." She laughed. "It was all part of the negotiation."

They ate in silence for a moment. He took a sip of his wine. "I'm not surprised. I know how persuasive you can be. No wonder your brothers have you running the office. You're a natural."

"At running things?"

"It does seem to be a particular talent of yours."

Her nose wrinkled. "I'm not sure if that's a compliment or not."

"I meant it as one."

She refilled their glasses. "Think I can persuade you to answer my question?"

Oh, boy. Here it comes. She was going to grill him about last night after all.

"Depends on the question, I guess."

She looked at him as if he'd said something stupid. "The one I asked a few minutes ago. What are we doing…officially?"

He hesitated, and she stood and grabbed the dishes. "I'll give you a minute. I need to get a sweater."

"Let's move this inside. It's getting chilly out here." He'd learned that no matter how warm the days might be in Texas this time of year, the nights cooled down in a hurry. A lot like the Iraqi desert at night.

He pushed that unexpected memory aside in a hurry. They cleared the table and took everything—including Sarge—into the house. Belle loaded the dishwasher while he put the lasagna in the fridge. By the time they went back into the living room, the dog was snoring like a buzz saw in his crate.

Jack and Belle settled onto the sofa, and he knew she was still waiting on an answer. He pulled her in close and kissed her temple.

"We went from pretending to reality pretty fast," he said. "And the reality is…really great. I definitely wasn't looking for anything serious." She raised her head, and he smiled into her wide blue eyes. Ocean eyes. Eyes that could easily sweep him under if he wasn't careful. He put his finger under her chin. "All I know is I like having you here. I like falling asleep with you. I like waking up with you. I like coming home to you." He rolled his eyes pointedly at the rug. "I even like it when you surprise me…to a point." Where was he going with this? He shared the startling—to him at least—truth. "Belle, I don't think *like* is a big enough word for what I feel. But it's all I can give you at the moment." He kissed her pillow-soft lips. "You need to know this isn't casual for me. It's… it's something more."

Her eyes shimmered as she looked up at him. "I'm glad to hear you say that. Because I'm falling for you, Jack Radcliffe. Falling hard. And fast. But that doesn't make my feelings any less real. I'm way past *like* when it comes to you." She kissed him. He cupped her head and returned it. He wasn't sure what *falling for him* meant exactly. It was as if she knew what he was ready to hear, and what might scare him off. He wasn't an idiot, though. He understood the meaning of *way past like*.

The kiss deepened, and he pulled her onto his lap. She wrapped her arms around his neck and made a little purring sound. The sound sent pleasure through his veins like whiskey, warming him from the inside with a burn that felt so good.

They ended up in the bedroom. In bed. Naked. He stared down at her as they moved together. She whispered his name, clutching at him, then crying out as they came together. Jack made some unintelligible growling sound, then collapsed on her. She made him feel things he'd never felt before. He was falling for her, too. Completely. Scary or not, he'd also moved *way past like*.

They lay together, warm, cozy and relaxed.

His head was propped against the tall headboard. Her head was resting on his chest. Her fingers, as usual, were tracing lightly across his skin. Branding him. Burning him.

"You should move in." He spoke his thoughts out loud. "Officially."

She didn't even look up. "Okay."

For some reason, he felt he had to clarify the statement she'd agreed to so easily. "It makes sense. You said your hotel suite is closing in on you. It's the same distance from the office to here as the hotel. There's plenty of room here, and let's face it, you're already making it your own."

Belle looked up, one eyebrow arched. "You just took a nice invitation and made it sound like a business transaction. Are you looking for a lover or a roommate?"

"Sorry. Like you said, we went from idle to full speed in a heartbeat." And now she *was* his heartbeat. "Maybe I'm overselling it or making excuses to myself. You asked earlier what we were officially. I think what I'm trying to say is that I want us *officially* together. Here." He gave her a quick squeeze. "Everywhere."

Chapter Ten

Belle let out a long, slow breath and kissed the skin directly over his heart. She could feel his pulse against her lips. *Together.* She didn't expect him to say anything different, but it was still a relief to hear him confirm it. They were together. A couple. Lovers. In love.

No, he *hadn't* said that. And neither had she...at least not out loud. But she *was* falling in love with Jack. She was sure of it. This wasn't some childish crush. It was more than her seeing her friends and family falling happily in love and thinking, *I want that.* This was a feeling she'd never had before. She shuddered.

"Hey," Jack said softly. "Are you cold? Grab the blankets, babe."

"You keep me warm enough." She grinned up at him as his eyes fell closed. "Is it just me, or does it feel like we've been together forever? Everything feels so normal between us."

He opened one eye. "There is nothing *normal* about us. What we just did was way better than normal."

"I'm not talking about *that*, you perv. I'm talking about the way we're so comfortable with each other. It doesn't feel like any other relationship I've been in. None of the awkward feeling that I have to be on my best behavior all the time. And I don't get the feeling that you're trying to impress me..." She raised her head and laughed, stopping his objection. "Except in bed, of course. You're very impressive there.

"I mean the way we talk with each other." She tried to think of a way to describe it. "It's natural. Organic. Like we belong, you know?"

"Yeah, I guess. We fit together nicely." He looked down at her. "And I'm not talking about sex." His eyes went to the Ansel Adams prints on the wall. "You know my taste. I like those."

She knew she'd taken a big chance with her shopping spree that afternoon. But the room felt firmly in the twenty-first century now. Callum had loaned Jack a work crew last week to pull up the mauve carpeting in the great room to reveal the wood floor beneath, and they'd removed the mirrored tiles from the wall, too.

"I'm glad you like the prints. I probably shouldn't have sprung it on you like I did, but I thought…" She paused, unsure about confessing the reasoning behind her shopping spree. It was more than a day of retail therapy. She'd had a goal in mind.

"Thought what? That it would be easier to beg forgiveness than permission?"

She chuckled, resting her chin on his chest to look into his warm, dark eyes. "Well, that *did* cross my mind, but I did this for you. I thought maybe if the place felt more like home that you'd be able to relax here. Be less stressed." *Stop having nightmares*.

"What do you mean *stressed*?" She saw the answer dawn in his eyes, which quickly cooled. "Are you talking about last night? Belle…"

"I thought a warmer, cozier surrounding might help your anxiety."

"Anxiety?" He sat higher, and she was forced to release her hold on him. He scowled at her. "So now you're psychoanalyzing me?"

She sat up and put her hand flat on his chest, where her head had rested a moment ago. "That

wasn't a diagnosis. But you're clearly having anxious moments in your sleep, even when you're not
having a flat-out nightmare." She swallowed hard,
trying to sound comforting and not condescend-
ing. "You've been through a lot of—"

"Don't pretend you know what I've been
through." His voice was hard. Cold. Where was
this anger coming from?

"I only meant that, in the span of a couple
months, you got out of the service and moved to
a new place. Started a new job. Got a house. Got
a dog. Got a roommate." She winked, hoping to
break through his sudden foul mood. "That's a lot
of change in a short time. I thought if I made the
house, this room, feel more comfortable, that it
would help you feel settled here."

At first his expression didn't change, then he
slowly—almost reluctantly—started to relax. The
lines around his eyes eased. His gaze softened.
His mouth went from a hard line to a gentle slant.

"You have a big heart, Belle."

And it's all yours.

"I care about you. If you can't talk to me about
whatever's haunting you, maybe you should find
someone else to talk to?"

He shook his head, but his half smile stayed in
place. "Let it go. I have a feeling that's not easy for
you to do, but you gotta let it go. Please."

"Harper said you won some sort of medal over there." His sister said he'd never told her the details or answered her questions about it. Maybe if Belle could get him talking about the more positive experiences in the military, like earning medals, his tension would ease.

But it backfired. His entire body stiffened. His heart rate changed beneath her fingertips, racing and jumping.

"Enough." His voice stayed level, but brooked no argument. "I never should have mentioned that to Harper, and I will never discuss it with you." He reached out to cup her cheek. "I'm doing you a favor by not talking about it. I know you think you're helping, but…don't. You being here helps me more than you'll ever know."

This man was hurting. And talking made him hurt even more right now. Belle was used to getting her way, but this was one time when she was going to have to stand down. For Jack's sake. At least for now. She leaned into his hand.

"I'm right here. And I'm not going anywhere."

The clouds lifted from his eyes. He drew her in for an intense kiss. "Thank God."

Jack wasn't sure what to expect when Belle asked if she could invite her brothers to the house for a barbecue that weekend. He understood the concept of meeting the family, but hers was a family unlike any he'd known. She'd invited Harper and Brady, too. As a safety buffer? Or as a nice way to complete the family circle between the Radcliffes and the Fortunes?

Of course, he'd agreed. After all, it was *her* home, too. She'd packed up her things from the Hotel Fortune and claimed half the walk-in closet—and the closet in one of the other bedrooms. And she'd been right when she'd said things felt natural between them.

Their schedules clicked—he was a morning person, so he made breakfast while she got herself going, and she was a night owl, so she handled dinner. They shared light housework and laundry in the evenings. They were in tune with each other. She knew when he needed a little space. He knew when she needed a trip to the shopping center, or a good foot rub while she was stretched out on the sofa. They liked the same shows on television, and—to his surprise—she was a sports fan, too. Not hard core, but she especially liked college sports. They were already talking trash about which teams would go the furthest in the March college championships.

It was a good life they were building. And now her brothers were arriving to check it out. Check *him* out. Sarge barreled toward the door to greet

Beau and Draper. Jack followed a little less enthu-
siastically, but he made sure a smile was firmly
planted on his face. For Belle's sake.

Brady and Harper arrived a few minutes later,
without the children. Brady's sister, Arabella, and
her husband, Jay, were babysitting the twins and
Christina.

Harper gave him a sly smile when he asked
about the kids. "Sometimes, Mommy and Daddy
want to be grown-ups, with the ability to drink
and laugh without always being on the lookout for
trouble. I love the twins, but they're very...lively."

Brady started laughing. "Just say it, hon.
They're freakin' exhausting."

Everyone gathered on the veranda, where Jack
was getting ready to throw steaks on the grill.
Belle was still in the kitchen, working on a huge
pot of jambalaya. She told him she'd learned the
dish from her grandmother, who'd grown up near
the bayou. As far as Jack could tell, it required
about a hundred different ingredients, but man, it
smelled good. Harper went in to help as soon as
everyone had a drink in their hand.

Conversation flowed surprisingly well. Jack
didn't know what to expect from two wealthy investment brokers from New Orleans, but Beau and
Draper weren't in the least bit snobbish. Drinking
beer and wearing jeans, they admired the potential

of the big house and approved of the work done so far. And when Sarge flung himself onto his back for belly scratches, they obliged him with a laugh.

"I can see why you brought this guy home," Draper said. "He's a character."

"To say the very least." Jack shook his head. "He's also a master thief. At first it was his own toys, so I didn't care as much. He's stashing his tennis balls somewhere. I have to give him a new one every day, because they keep vanishing. But now he's turned his attention to Belle's stuff. She's had three shoes go missing this week."

Beau laughed. "I pity the dog if he's going after Belle's shoes. That girl loves her footwear, and none of it is cheap."

"On the other hand—" Draper held up his finger to make his point "—it'll give her an excuse for more shopping, which our girl loves even more than shoes." The two brothers clinked their beer bottles together in a toast.

"You make her sound materialistic, and that's not the Belle I know." Jack turned from the grill to face them. "And she's a woman, not a girl."

There was a beat of silence. Brady let out a slow whistle and picked up Sarge's tennis ball of the day, heading out to the yard and away from the sudden tension on the veranda.

"You gotta understand," Beau said, "she's our

baby sister, so we can't help seeing her as that little princess who used to run around demanding we sit for her tea parties. And we *did*. Because what Tinkerbelle wanted, she got. Even as a five-year-old."

Draper looked straight at Beau. "Jack's right. Belle's not a five-year-old playing princess anymore. For crying out loud, she manages our entire office. And I told you before, she doesn't want to be called Tinkerbelle. It's time for us to see her the way Jack does. Well…" He shuddered. "Not quite the way Jack does, but as an adult."

"Fair enough." Beau took a swig of beer. "But you gotta admit that *woman* loves to shop."

"For others as much as herself," Draper countered.

Jack had to agree. He nodded toward the house. "Pretty much everything you see in this place has her touch on it—whether it was advice or if she went out and bought it."

"That sounds right," Beau answered. "She likes giving as much as getting." He turned to Draper. "Remember how mad Mom used to get at her when she'd take stuff outside and just hand it to random strangers?"

Draper tipped his head back and laughed. "I forgot about that!" He turned to Jack. "It started with her toys. She was probably six or seven. She decided she had too many so she'd take toys out front and hand them to people walking by. Dad told her to at least set up a table and *sell* them, but she refused. It was adorable when it was her own stuff. Mom told us it showed Belle's generous spirit."

Beau nodded. "Then Belle decided we *all* had too much, and she started trying to give away things that didn't belong to her. My baseball glove. Savannah's riding boots. We usually caught her in time, and Mom still defended her, saying we did have too much."

Draper chuckled. "Until the day Mom saw Belle out there trying to hand an antique porcelain vase to some stranger on the sidewalk! Mom was done after that, generous spirit or not." Draper shook his head at the memory. "Belle was grounded for two weeks and ordered not to give anything to anyone without Mom's approval."

The brothers laughed together and started talking about some other story from their childhood in New Orleans. Jack set the steaks on the grill and the sizzle sent up an enticing aroma. Belle had lectured that, if he insisted on serving steak with jambalaya, it had to be one with Cajun seasoning, so she'd whipped up a bowl of spices last night to use as a rub—paprika, cayenne, garlic, oregano and more. They'd rubbed it into the steaks before everyone arrived, so even the smoke had a kick to it.

Kind of like the woman who made it. The

woman with a heart so huge she'd given things away to total strangers as a child. That story had kicked him hard. As if he wasn't already falling in love with her. He straightened. Maybe it was the Cajun spice swirling around in his chest.

Nope. It was the NOLA woman who was making him sweat. And making him fall in love.

"Yowza, that is some kind of spicy!" Harper slammed down the lid on the pot of jambalaya and blinked.

"Too much?" Belle asked as she set the pan of corn bread on the counter. "My brothers won't think so, but I forgot not everyone is from New Orleans."

"Brady will devour it. I'll give it a try, but it's good to know there's steak, too."

"Umm…" Belle winced. "It's cajun steak."

Harper laughed. Her laughter was so much quicker than her brother's.

"At least tell me there's no cayenne in that corn bread."

"I promise this is totally cayenne-free. And if you want, I have leftover lemon chicken from last night. I'll be glad to warm a plate for you."

Harper turned, putting her hand on her hip. "Okay, how did my surly baby brother find a sweetheart like you?"

"I have six older siblings—trust me, I'm not always sweet."

"I can't imagine that large of a family. It was only Jack and me growing up. After our parents died, it was *really* just the two of us."

Belle could smell the steaks cooking outside, so she started cutting the corn bread into squares.

"Was Jack always so serious?" She didn't think of him as surly. Solemn, maybe. Which made her appreciate his smiles even more.

"He's been everything at one point or another." Harper started ladling the shrimp, crawfish and rice into the large bowl Belle had set near the stove. "He was a class clown as a kid. He was in high school when Mom and Dad were killed in the accident, and he was angry for a while after that. He told me at graduation that he was going to 'take some time.'" She made air quotes, laughing when some rice flew off the spoon she was juggling. "He did two semesters of college, decided it wasn't for him, and started picking up different construction jobs. Then one day out of the blue, he called to say he'd joined the Army. He seemed happy. Grown-up."

"And when he came home?"

Harper shrugged. "He's definitely quieter now. He's adjusting to a lot of changes while he's transitioning to civilian life." She nudged Belle's shoulder as they headed out to the veranda with dinner. "He's lucky to have you to help him with that."

They joined the men outside and sat down to the feast. Her brothers were thrilled to have a taste of their hometown. Harper was okay with the steak. She grabbed a few shrimp from Brady's plate and fanned herself after every bite.

It was nice to see everyone laughing together like a family. Even Jack chuckled a few times in that low, almost reluctant way he had. Like he felt bad that he thought something was funny. She knew he'd been a little nervous about hosting her brothers. He hadn't said so, but she could see it in his eyes and the way his body had been so tense. But now he was leaning back in his chair, holding a beer and smiling at the conversation swirling around the table.

This was a typical Fortune gathering—chaotic, funny, competitive and loving. Brady was cut from the same cloth as her brothers, of course, and he waded right into the noisy debate on which city had the best football teams. Harper was more like Jack—happy to observe the mayhem rather than jump into it. She looked across the table at Belle.

"Were your family meals always like this?"

"Sometimes." Belle refilled her and Harper's wineglasses. "Mom never let things get too out of hand if we were in the formal dining room, but if we were eating in the kitchen or on the patio, she usually just let us go. Especially once we reached adulthood. I think she figured her job was done by that point, and we were on our own, as long as no food or utensils went airborne."

"And your dad?"

Belle laughed before taking a sip of her wine. "He worked really long hours, especially when we were kids, and a lot of times he'd head into his home office after dinner." She winked. "Probably to get away from us! When he'd had enough, he'd say so, and we listened. Dad's a man of few words, but people listen when he speaks."

Harper looked at Jack. "Sounds like my brother...a man of few words."

He rolled his eyes. "Yeah, but when I speak, no one listens."

Belle rested her elbow on the table and put her chin on her hand, blinking her eyes playfully. "I always listen to you, sweetheart."

His mouth slanted into a grin, and a flicker of heat shone in his eyes.

"When I can get a word in edgewise, babe."

Harper put her hands over her heart. "Stop it! You're too cute together!"

The men paused their debate and turned to face Jack and Belle. Beau raised his glass in a toast. "To our lovey-dovey host and hostess. Jack—get used to your girlfriend getting her way, because that's her superpower. And, sis, you picked a good guy."

Draper raised his glass in agreement. "So much better than Chad."

Belle muttered a curse, but Jack barely raised an eyebrow.

"Chad?"

Beau laughed. "Chad was the worst. He was Belle's lesson that sometimes people will do anything for Fortune money or influence. We've all had at least one of those. Goes with the territory, I guess. Belle had hers early—in high school. Chad fawned all over her just because he wanted to say he was hanging out with the Fortunes. But did Belle listen when we warned her? No-o-o."

Draper chimed in, ignoring the daggers Belle was throwing his way. "Belle's always been in love with love. That's why we have to watch out for her…" His voice trailed off.

Belle wasn't the only one glaring at him. Jack was, too. She put her hand on his. Her brothers could be idiots and they refused to let her grow up, but they meant well. And Chad *had* been a gold digger at heart.

Draper cleared his throat loudly. "I mean…we *used* to watch out for her. When she was a kid. Which she clearly is not anymore. She's a grown woman, and she's making her own choices." Belle had to bite her lip to keep from laughing as her brother tried to save himself. He pointed at Jack. "You're a very good choice. Of Belle's." Draper finally composed himself. "Look, the truth is we'll always look out for our sister. It's good to know you're doing the same. You've got her back, and that's all Beau and I need to know."

Jack looked at her and nodded. "I've got her back. And I think she has mine."

"You know I do."

"Oh, my God," Harper said, her eyes shining. "I'm going to need tissues if you two don't cut it out. You're adorable!"

Jack grinned and tugged on Belle's hand. She slid onto his lap, sliding her arms around his neck. He spoke just to her, ignoring the exaggerated groans from everyone else.

"Did you hear that? We're adorable."

"I heard. But I already knew that." She kissed him. It was meant to be a quick, sweet kiss, but started heating up the moment they connected.

"And *that's* our cue to go." Beau laughed.

Belle jumped up from Jack's lap. "No! We have dessert!"

Draper arched a brow at her as he rose to leave. "Looked like you started dessert without us."

Chapter Eleven

"Can you explain to me how the homeowner is going to get into this walk-in closet?" Marcus stood in front of a pocket doorway that had been fully framed in. Jack stood back, watching the conversation. The quality of the framing wasn't the problem. The location was. It was directly behind where the vanity would be.

Tucker Landmire, a young carpentry apprentice, hung his head.

"I guess I misread the marks on the floor."

"The marks on the *floor*? Did you look at the actual *floor plan*?" Tucker shook his head and Marcus groaned. "That's why I leave a copy here every morning—so everyone can double-check *before* they make a mistake."

Jack stepped forward when he heard the edge in Marcus's voice. "The good news is we caught it before the drywall team got started. Tucker will get a good lesson in *re*framing a doorway." Jack gave the kid a quick smile. "And I'm guessing this is a mistake he'll never make again. Right, Tucker?"

"Yes, sir. I mean…no, sir, I won't do it again."

He was nineteen. Tall, skinny and awkward—a kid who hadn't quite grown into his own body yet. He was shy and sometimes failed to ask questions when he was unsure, but he was a hardworking kid and he really wanted to learn. He was going to make a fine carpenter someday. Not necessarily right now.

Tucker started ripping out his half day's work, and Marcus and Jack walked through the rest of the house, making sure there weren't any more surprises. They went over the checklist together, making sure everything was ordered properly. Working with Fortune Brothers Construction made that less of a worry. They were used to building commercial projects, so the Fortunes ran a tight ship.

Jack gave Marcus a ride home that night because his coworker's truck was in the shop again. Marcus buckled in, grumbling to Jack, "I don't know why Callum wants you working with me on another house. You're ready."

"I asked him to," Jack confessed. "I'm not sure I want to be in charge of a team."

Marcus directed Jack to turn into an older development of small brick ranches on tidy, tree-lined streets. "I'm guessing that has something to do with whatever happened overseas?" Marcus pointed to a humble but tidy house with a single garage and a small front porch. Jack kept his expression neutral as he pulled into the drive, but inwardly he flinched at the memory of what his so-called leadership skills had led to.

"I don't know if I'm cut out to be a leader."

"Bull." Marcus turned to face him when the truck stopped. "You handled that kid Tucker better than I did. You know how to get guys to want to do the right thing. That's a talent that can't be taught. Have you talked to your girl about your service yet?"

Jack chewed the inside of his cheek. "I told her a little."

"Uh-huh." Marcus rolled his eyes. "You got a woman you like, and she likes you back. Don't blow it, Jack."

Time for a subject change.

"You have family nearby?"

"Yeah. My daughter and her family are down

in Houston. My boys are both out on the West Coast. One's married. One's divorced and having fun playing the field."

"Grandkids?"

Marcus nodded. "Seven altogether. Only two in Texas. I try to see those two as much as I can, but my daughter and I are still rebuilding trust after all those years I wasted at the bottom of a bottle."

Jack looked through the windshield at the simple home. "So you're alone a lot."

Marcus snorted. "Trust me, I'm better off alone. Even sober, I'm too honest for a lot of folk."

"What about a pet?" Jack thought of a raggedy, angry black cat sitting in a cage at the shelter.

"A *pet*? I don't need some damn animal destroying my place or bugging me for attention." He paused, then shook his head, rejecting the idea. "Besides, what sweet little creature would want to live with an old turd like me?"

Jack watched Marcus head inside. He couldn't help thinking that Diva wouldn't bug Marcus for attention—she'd *demand* it. But not all the time. She was a queen after all, regardless of her tattered ear and scarred lip. He headed home, thinking about some of the other pets at the shelter, and wondering if there was a way that lonely veterans could be matched with the animals no one wanted. Veterans knew what it felt like to be isolated and different.

He mentioned the idea to Belle over dinner, admitting he had no idea how to do it. They were out on the veranda—their favorite dinner spot when the weather was warm enough. Sarge was snoring at Jack's feet.

"I think you've already discovered a way to do it," Belle said. "You've got a connection with the rescue group, so you know which animals are available. If you can figure out a way to get to know some of the veterans in town, you could match them up yourself. Oh, wait…" She brightened. "My cousin Nicole is married to a soldier. Collin might be able to hook you up with local veterans."

"That sounds like a big project. On top of my full-time job. And you."

She waved her fork in his direction. "Do not add me to a list of tasks, mister. I'm not some burden on your time. I'm your…" Her eyes widened. "Girlfriend?"

"At the very least."

The words were out before he could think about what he was saying. The soft pink rising on her cheeks told him it was too late to take them back. He knew what Belle was to him, but he wasn't prepared to say the words out loud yet.

"I mean…" He struggled, much to her apparent amusement.

"What *do* you mean, Jack?"

"*Girlfriend* sounds so juvenile. We're not in high school. We're…we're more than that, don't you think?" He reached out to take her hand. Definitely more. She was becoming his everything.

Her smile was warm, losing its teasing edge. "I agree *girlfriend* is juvenile, and *lover* is…I don't know…gross?" She rushed to explain, "There's nothing gross about actually *being* lovers, but it's not how I want to introduce you to people. *Paramour* is a fancy way of saying *lover.* And *good friend* sounds like *roommate*."

"Friends with benefits?"

She laughed, gathering their empty dishes together. "I can see it now… Dad, this is Jack, my friend with benefits."

"Your dad is coming to Rambling Rose?"

"That was just a hypothetical, but my parents will visit eventually. My brothers put them off for a few months to get the office up and running smoothly." Her smile faded. "Does meeting my parents worry you?"

"I've already met your brothers and survived. I think I can handle your parents." They finished clearing the table and headed inside, Sarge hopping along next to them.

Jack was happy with Belle. At the same time, it felt like things were racing along between them. While he liked that, it also terrified him. He'd been in some scary situations, but falling in love was scary on a whole new level.

Belle set their dishes in the sink. Sarge came into the kitchen and went to his water dish. Stephanie had suggested they elevate Sarge's dishes so he didn't have to lean down with all his front weight on that one leg. Jack had made a wooden stand with holes to hold Sarge's food and water dishes securely at the right height. As usual, the more Sarge drank, the more water that went on the floor rather than in his mouth.

Jack grabbed the beach towel they kept nearby for that reason. He held one end, then used his foot to wipe the other end across the puddle on the floor. "I swear this dog has a hole in his mouth. Or he bites the water instead of drinking it." He shook his finger at Sarge. "You make a mess!"

Belle spun around from the sink. "Oh, my God—speaking of messes—I forgot to tell you! I solved the mystery of my missing shoes and the tennis balls. Follow me."

She led him down the hallway that accessed the spare bedrooms on the opposite side of the great room. He'd taken the door off the farthest room so he could replace it. The original hollow-core door had a hole in it where someone had kicked it.

Belle looked over her shoulder, grinning when she saw Sarge was following along with great interest. "The silly dog must have forgotten I was home, and he went slinking by the kitchen with one of my Jimmy Choos in his mouth. Instead of yelling, I followed him. The little thief came in here. Look in the closet." She pointed to the closet. He slid the doors open farther and his mouth fell open.

There was basically a nest in there. A giant pile of old drop cloths from painting, along with some furniture-moving blankets. And a huge stash of tennis balls and single, unmatched shoes. Jack looked at Belle.

"They don't look damaged?"

"They're not chewed at all," she said. "It's like he's just…saving them for some reason. Like a dragon maintains a hoard of treasure." Belle bent down to scratch Sarge's ears. "I'm grateful you didn't eat them, you terror, but you still can't keep them."

Stephanie agreed with Jack and Belle's laughing suggestion that Sarge's stash was a dragon hoard. They'd stopped back at the veterinary clinic after delivering a yowling Diva to Marcus. Jack had been honest with Belle that morning, admitting he was asking her to act as a shield, because Marcus couldn't tell him and the cat to go to hell if she was there. She didn't mind—anything to see Jack in action with his pet adoption idea.

The older man had definitely looked like he wanted to throw them out, whether Belle was there in his living room or not. Until Jack lifted Diva out of the carrier and handed her over to Marcus. Man and cat had taken one look at each other and, if not love at first sight, there was at least fascination. Marcus eventually cleared his throat and made a face at the cat.

"You look like you've been through some things, lady. But then again, so have I."

He'd kept the cat, insisting it was for a trial period, and accepted the supplies—food, litter pan, collar—only if he could pay for them. So Jack and Belle stopped back at the clinic to give the money to Stephanie for the Paws and Claws rescue. That's when Belle told Stephanie about Sarge's closet treasure trove.

"Think about it," Stephanie said. "We don't think Sarge had a great life before he was injured—it's very possible he was abused or neglected. The surgeon said when they did the amputation that the injury could have been from a kick as well as an accident."

"I hate to even think about that," Belle said, her heart aching. "He's such a sweet dog."

Jack didn't speak, but the set of his jaw spoke volumes. The idea of the dog suffering at the hands of another person burned them all.

Stephanie nodded. "After Sarge was living at the rescue shelter for months, Jack comes in and changes the dog's world completely. A big house. A big yard. A person who loves him." She patted Jack's shoulder. "As much as Sarge adores you, it's possible he still thinks you and all those tennis balls might disappear someday. That it's too good to be true. My hunch is he's saving things as his own secret stash of touchstones, just in case."

Jack and Belle stared at each other. The thought that Sarge was so terrified of losing them that he was hoarding their things absolutely broke her heart. Jack took her hand, and she felt tears welling in her eyes.

"That is so damn sad!"

"Well—" Stephanie smiled "—the bright side is that Sarge is clearly very happy. He just needs a little time to build his faith in you."

Jack took Belle's hand. "I don't care how many tennis balls he steals, but I'm not sure how many shoes Belle can live without."

Belle laughed. "I have plenty where those came from. You haven't even seen half my shoe collec-

tion." Many were still in New Orleans. "As long
as he avoids chewing them, maybe Sarge and I can
come to a compromise about how many he actually needs in there to feel secure."

When they arrived home, Sarge greeted them
at the door. His enthusiasm for their arrival may
have had something to do with the bag of Chinese
takeout they were carrying. Belle knelt and hugged
the wiggling, smiling dog. "You and I need to talk
about boundaries, mister. But I feel like I understand you a little better." Jack looked down at her
with an odd expression. Still on her knees with
Sarge, she asked, "What's wrong?"

He shook his head. "Nothing. This is another
one of those normal moments. Coming home together." He held up the bag of takeout. "Greeted
by our dog. Dinner in hand. It's…nice." His eyes
were saying something more than *nice*, but she
didn't press him. The moment was too sweet to
ruin by pushing him. She was pretty sure he was
falling in love as fast as she was.

Jack had another bad dream that night. Belle
woke as soon as he started twitching. Pretty soon
he was mumbling words she couldn't understand,
his head turning back and forth in distress. He
was sweating as he tossed and turned. Then he
went silent, which was always worse. His breath-

ing was ragged. Uneven. She wanted to wake him, but didn't want to scare him. A sob caught in his throat, and she knew she had to try. She rested her hand lightly on his shoulder.

"It's okay, Jack. You're safe." She repeated the whispered words a few times, and his breathing began to level out. His eyes opened, and he looked around as if he didn't recognize the room. When he saw her watching him, his expression fell.

"Another dream?" he asked.

"Jack, you have to tell me what the nightmares are about. Is it the war? Something from your childhood?" He tried to pull his shoulder away from her touch, but she wouldn't let go. "Jack, we agreed to have an honest relationship, and you're not telling me everything."

"There are some things that people don't talk about, Belle." His voice was hard. "Are you telling me you've told me everything?"

She sat up, staring down at him in the dark.

"I'll tell you whatever you want to know."

"Fine—what scares you the most? And why?"
Losing you...because I love you.

She swallowed hard, steeling herself for the test he was giving her.

"Snakes. I don't like the way they move. Creeps me out. Next question?"

"Did you ever have a pet die? Tell me about it."

Oh, he was playing hardball now. Asking her about things he knew she wouldn't want to discuss—that no one wanted to talk about. It was a challenge. And Belle Fortune didn't back down from challenges.

"I had a cat when I was little." She blew out a long breath. "His name was Pepper. He was black-and-white. He used to sleep on my bed every night, on a pillow right next to mine." She blinked at the memory. "I was twelve when he got cancer. I cried for a month after he died." She lifted her chin defiantly, refusing to cave. "Next question?"

"Tell me about the first time you had sex."

Good thing it was dark, because she was sure her cheeks were flaming. But she'd said she'd tell him anything he wanted to know.

"Chad Remington." She wrinkled her nose at the memory. "We were seniors in high school. It was after a football game. His parents were out of town, so we went to his place. There was a lot of fumbling involved, and I'm not talking about the football game."

"Wait…" He sat up next to her, leaning back against the headboard. "The same Chad your brothers said used you to get closer to your family?"

"That's the one." She shifted to face him. "They

do *not* know that part of the story, so don't you dare say anything."

"Did he pressure you?"

"Why? Are you going to go find him and beat him up?" She shook her head before leaning into his side. She needed his warmth, and he obliged, wrapping his arm around her. "I was eighteen. I knew what I was doing. Well, neither of us knew what we were doing, but it was definitely consensual. And Chad wasn't as bad as Beau and Draper said. Sure, he was all agog over the Fortune name and our fancy house and all that, but he wasn't a sociopath or anything. He liked me. Eventually I realized I would never be as important to him as the house and the cars and the lifestyle."

They sat in silence. Jack had run out of curiosity. She glanced up.

"That's three questions asked and answered, buster. Now it's your turn."

He stiffened.

"I'm sorry, Belle." He smoothed his hand over her head, then kissed the same spot. "I'm sorry for being such a jackass with those questions just now. That was uncalled-for." He kissed the top of her head again. His lips stayed pressed there for a moment. "I'm sorry because…I still can't tell you what you think you want to know."

"What I *think* I want to know?" She sat up

abruptly. "This may come as a shock to you, but I'm usually very sure about what I want. And what I want is an honest relationship."

"You're always sure of what you want, babe." His eyes were wide and sad. "But I'm not going to do it. I'm protecting you."

"I don't need your protection, damn it." She pushed his arm away. "I'm not some cartoon princess. I'm a grown woman. I want us to be honest with each other." She leaned in close, staring straight into his dark, troubled eyes. "It has to be a two-way street."

"And if it's not a two-way street? If you don't get what you want for once?"

"That's not fair."

"Come here." Jack pulled her back close to his side with a heavy sigh. She wanted to resist, but couldn't. She loved him and he was in pain. Jack's whole body relaxed at her touch. "I didn't mean it that way. You're a force of nature, but you're not bossy. Much." She felt him shake with a soft huff of laughter at his own joke. "I just meant…can you accept what I can give you and know that it's as much as I'm capable of sharing? That I'm doing my best?" There was a pleading in his voice that touched the softest part of her heart. He'd never sounded this vulnerable before. He spoke again.

"I'm giving you more than I've given anyone. I'm giving you my heart. Can't that be enough?"

She stopped breathing. Did he say what she thought he'd said?

"I mean it, Belle. I'm falling for you. Hell, I've already fallen. Just because I can't share a few dark corners of my life, that doesn't mean I don't care for you. A lot." He rested his cheek on her head. "I hope that's good enough, because I can't imagine my life without you in it."

She didn't move. It felt like he needed as much physical connection as possible right now. She whispered the words she'd been holding on to, breathing them across his chest softly.

"I love you, Jack."

He didn't respond. That was okay. The words weren't really meant for him to hear anyway. She just couldn't hold them inside any longer. She spoke louder, wanting to be sure he heard the next part. "As long as you're giving me as much as you're capable of giving, it'll be enough." She pressed a quick kiss against his skin.

"So…we're really doing this, huh?" He hooked his finger under her chin and lifted her head so they could see each other. "We're doing the fall-for-each-other thing? All the way?" He was saying everything *but* that he loved her.

"Looks that way." She grinned. "Nervous?"

"Terrified. And not scared at all. That's weird, right?"

"Not for us. Sounds just about perfect."

The kiss started softly, full of emotion and tender hope for a future together. A future neither of them had anticipated, so they had no idea what it might look like. The kiss quickly deepened, with all the passion she knew would guide them. No matter what the future held, she was walking toward it with Jack at her side. And if he had to keep a few secrets, that was okay. At least for now.

Chapter Twelve

"Did I tell you what that darn cat did?" Marcus laughed as he and Jack headed into the house that was now fully drywalled and ready for finishing. Today's project was the kitchen, and cupboards were lined up in the hallway.

"What did Diva do now?" Every day brought a new story about the cat. How smart she was. How acrobatic she was. How silly she was.

"She figured out not only how to climb on top of the refrigerator but now she can open the cupboard doors up there, and she hides inside. She bats the door so it opens and closes over and over." Marcus puffed up like a proud dad, even though he was describing mayhem. "Two o'clock in the morning, and I'm hearing this soft *thump, thump, thump*. I tore the house apart trying to find the source, till I caught sight of a furry paw coming out of the highest cupboard. I swear, she did it just to get me out of a sound sleep. It's like she's not my cat at all. It's more like I'm her servant."

Jack nodded, asking the same question he always asked, "Want me to take her back to the shelter?"

And sure enough, he got the same answer he'd heard for a week. "Hell, no! I'm the only fool who'd put up with that ugly cat."

Marcus had a neighbor who was also a veteran. He wanted Jack to find the woman a special cat or maybe a small dog.

"Marcia's a petite thing, like your girl. And she's had some health issues." Marcus took a box cutter to the boxes the kitchen cupboards were in.

Jack started dragging the lower cabinets into place, ignoring the little catch in his heart at the words *like your girl*. He did a mental inventory of the animals he'd seen at the shelter. "There might be an older animal that would fit the bill. Does she have a lot of kids running around?"

"Kids?" Marcus snorted. "She's my age and divorced. She has a daughter and a couple grandkids, but they're up north somewhere."

"So she's alone, huh?" Jack gave him a wink. "Maybe what she needs is a *neighbor* to comfort her." He laughed when Marcus flipped his middle finger at him. "Okay, okay. But what kind of health problems? A pet won't work if she's in and out of the hospital a lot…"

He really needed to come up with a list of questions if he was going to match any more veterans with animals. Because after seeing how happy Sarge was, and how happy Marcus and Diva were together, it made Jack want to do more.

"It's nothing like that." Marcus reached into his toolbox for a larger screwdriver. "Marcia's fine now, but she had back surgery last year. I offered to mow her lawn for her last summer, and we got to know each other."

Jack decided not to say out loud what he was thinking—that Marcus seemed to know an awful lot about this single lady neighbor of his. "I'll check out some of the animals that are tougher to adopt out and see if there's a good fit."

The work crew came in and they all worked until lunchtime. The crew ate inside, Jack outside. Jack understood that the easiest way for the crew to bond was to laugh at or complain about the boss. They couldn't do that if he was sitting right there. Besides, the hot sun didn't bother him much. He'd seen worse.

Marcus joined him outside with his lunch pail. "So what did your girl pack for lunch today?"

"Looks like…" Jack peeled back the white parchment paper Belle wrapped his sandwich in. "Creole shrimp salad on a ciabatta roll. And some cookies from that coffee shop she likes in town."

"She's spoiling you rotten, man. You know that, right?"

He couldn't argue. Life had been pretty sweet since they'd declared they were falling for each other. Whatever that meant. Belle had reorganized the kitchen and made it her own, even if it was still awash in 1980s dusty rose. She'd started packing lunches for him—usually some sort of reimagined leftovers from dinner. The shrimp salad started as last night's grilled kebabs.

Jack hadn't told her yet, but Callum's architect was drawing up a couple of options to remodel the kitchen. Of course, Jack couldn't do anything until he figured out a way to afford to buy the house. Callum said he'd give him a fair price on it. Probably a price Belle could put on her exclusive black credit card, but that wasn't going to happen.

"Things getting serious with you two?" Marcus asked.

"I think so, yeah." Jack took a bite of his sandwich. "She's moved in. We've entertained her brothers and got their stamp of approval. The dog loves her. And so do I."

Marcus's eyebrows shot up. "Really? The big *L*, eh? You tell her?"

"Not yet, but I told her I was…um…falling for her."

"And…?" Marcus gestured with his hands, as if to say *go on.*

"And she said she's falling for me, too." He grinned at his friend.

"And she knows about…what happened?"

Jack's smile vanished, and he shook his head sharply. "No. But we talked it through and she understands that I can't tell her everything. She's an open book. I'm not. She accepts that."

His stomach churned when he remembered that childish game he'd pulled the other night, pushing her to talk about uncomfortable things in *her* life in a ploy to make her leave *him* alone. It had been mean-spirited, and she'd known it. But, being Belle, she hadn't backed down. She was no quitter.

"She said that, huh? That she accepts it?" Marcus drained his drink. "Miss Belle Fortune doesn't strike me as the type to just accept things. She's more the bend-the-world-to-my-will type."

Jack coughed out a laugh. "She'd make a very good ruler of the world, but she's not inflexible. She's…determined. But it's not as much about getting her way as it is about her caring so much. About me."

Marcus tipped his head to the side. "So she cares about you. Maybe even loves you. And you think she's going to let this drop? Just like that?" He stood, brushing the dust off his pants before giving Jack a pointed look. "You should get it over with now, my friend. She'll get it out of you sooner or later."

What was it Jack had just said to himself? *She was no quitter.* But Belle really had seemed to accept things the way they were. She hadn't pouted about it. If anything, she'd been even more affectionate. More free with random hugs or a pat on his butt when she passed him in the hall. She'd started sending him cute little texts during the day. Sometimes a quick miss u, sometimes a few suggestive emojis for what might happen after dinner that night.

And nights had been better, too. They'd explored their physical attraction in new and creative ways. Hot and steamy. Slow and tender. Hot and tender. Slow and steamy. He smiled to himself as he followed Marcus back to work. Belle cared about him, whether he deserved it or not. Just as importantly, she accepted him as he was. Other than a few dark corners she didn't need to know about, they were fine. Better than fine. No matter what Marcus said, they were on their way to building a future together.

Belle shut down her computer and pushed the desk drawer closed a little more forcefully than she'd intended. Beau poked his head around the corner with his eyebrows raised.

"You okay out here?"

She wrinkled her nose. "Yes. I guess. I'm glad it's almost Friday."

He walked over to her desk and leaned against it, folding his arms across his chest. "Everything going okay with you and the construction guy?"

"Seriously? You've had dinner in our home and Jack's still *the construction guy* to you?"

He raised his hands. "I didn't mean it that way. Jack's a good guy. I like him. You're happy when you're with him. I like *that* even more." His hands dropped. "But when you're here at work? I don't see a lot of joy in you."

It was a fair observation, but she still defended herself. "This is an investment firm. I didn't know being joyful was a job requirement. I'm doing my job—"

"Of course you are. And you're fantastic at it. I'm not talking to you as a boss, though. I'm talking to you as your big brother. Something is off with you. So spill."

She chewed on her lip for a moment before answering. Beau seemed genuinely concerned, and he *had* stopped calling her Tinkerbelle all the time. "I promised when we moved here that I'd give you a year as office manager, but…I don't know if I can do this for a year. I love you both, but the job? Not so much."

His brows lowered. "What would you do? And what would we do without you?"

"I want to open a boutique here in Rambling Rose. I have a business plan. I have potential suppliers lined up. The more I think about it, the more I want to make the move sooner rather than later."

She and Jack had talked about it again last night. He was the first person to have seen her actual business plan. As she'd scrolled through the pages on her tablet, he'd let out a low whistle and asked her what she was waiting for. Then he'd grabbed his own tablet and pulled up a blueprint app. They'd spent a few hours playing around with possible floor plan ideas for a shop. Jack's support felt like lifting the gate in front of a racehorse. All she could think about now was how much she wanted to *run*.

Beau frowned. "Retail is risky now, sis."

She gestured around the office. "What's riskier than investing?" He grimaced, then nodded in agreement.

"Fair enough. But retail…there are so many things that can affect your bottom line. And the overhead…"

"Oh, you mean things like—" she ticked off the items on her fingers "—rent? Build-out? Inventory? Utilities? Ads? Website? Newsletters? Promotional events…" Beau started to interrupt, but she talked right over him. "And let's not forget about loss-leader items to bring customers into the store, markdowns and how they affect the profit and loss reports… Oh, and those pesky business taxes." She gave her brother a pointed look. "I'm hoping a couple investors I know can help with the accounting and financial planning end of things."

Beau gave her a reluctant grin. "You can be your own darn accountant. You're the most natural numbers person I've ever met." He sighed. "Okay, so you know what's involved. Have you—"

"Created a business plan and set a budget? Yes. I could use an investor or two, though."

Beau burst out laughing, pushing up to his feet. "Wait…not only do you want to quit you also want us to give you money so you *can* quit? Belle, you are definitely fearless!"

"I'm not quitting, at least not yet. But I don't think I'll last the year. I'm sorry." She gave him a playful shrug. "And if you don't want to invest, I can always ask Mom." It was often assumed that

Sarah Fortune married into wealth, but the truth was Miles Fortune was a self-made man, and Belle's mother came from money. Even now she handled her own investments.

Beau chuckled with a shake of his head. "Well, you're smart, that's for sure. Dad would be a hard sell on investing in a boutique, even for his spoiled baby girl." He reached out and tugged her ponytail. "But Mom is a different story. Listen, don't call anyone yet. Set up an appointment for you, Draper and me, and we'll listen to what you have to say. You're going to have to really sell it, 'cause I'm still not convinced on the idea of a retail biz."

As she drove home, she knew she'd made definite headway in her boutique plan. At the same time—and as much as she loved her family—it was frustrating that they still couldn't take her as seriously as she'd like. Yes, she was the baby of seven, but she was an adult now. With an excellent college education. That *baby* tag couldn't stick with her forever, could it? Her car alerted her to an incoming call from Shelly in New Orleans. She hit the button on her steering wheel to accept the call, thankful the top was up on the convertible.

"Hey, Shell! What's up?" She usually spoke to her friend every weekend, but it was only Thursday afternoon.

"Hi, girl! Mom just surprised me with tickets

for her and I to go to Manhattan this weekend for my birthday. Want to come with?"

Shelly was from old money and their pockets ran even deeper than the Fortunes. Shelly's family also had a slightly different work ethic, choosing to live off their inheritance rather than work. Though everyone was active in the family's charitable foundation.

Usually, Belle would have leaped at the chance to go shopping in New York, but not now.

"I can't this time, sorry. The timing's bad. But you and your mom have fun." Belle drove into the development where Jack's house—their house—was located. Some homes were still being kept up nicely, but others, like Jack's, had been neglected for a while. Her cousin Kane had convinced Callum to buy them up as soon as they hit the market and do what he called an "upflip." More than simple cosmetic improvements, their teams were rebuilding the homes from the studs out, modernizing them while still ensuring each one had a unique vibe. Fortune Brothers Construction was working to revive some of the older neighborhoods in town as well as adding new homes. It was all part of an agreement they'd come to with Rambling Rose locals to be better community partners.

"Aw…" Shelly's voice was pouty. "I was hoping you were ready for a break from dusty old

Texas. Can't your brothers live without you for a few days? Or is it the other man in your life you're worried about?"

Belle pulled into the driveway, then drove the BMW into the garage. "I'm not worried about him, but honestly, it's not a good time to leave. Thanks for the invite, though. Maybe next time, okay?"

Shelly let out a long sigh. "Belle Fortune turning down a week in Manhattan. I never thought I'd see the day. How are things going with Jack? You really think he's the one Madame Fauntegeaux was talking about?"

"The palm reader? I don't think Madame Fauntegeaux had much to do with it, but…yes. He's my guy, Shell— Oof!" Sarge barreled into her legs as she opened the door, making her stumble back. "Dog, you don't need to tackle me every time I come home." She walked over and opened the doors to the backyard so he could do his daily patrol for critters to chase. "Jack and I may not have officially declared our love for each other yet, but we have a house. And a dog. That's as real as it gets."

She kicked off her shoes and carried them down the hall, setting them up on the shoe rack Jack had built in the closet. High enough to be safe from Sarge.

Shelly didn't sound convinced. "Having a house

and a dog makes you roommates, not soul mates. Are you saying he finally opened up to you about those bad dreams? You said that was bugging you last week."

Belle sat on the edge of the bed, frowning at her reflection in the mirror. The framed rose picture she'd received at the hotel was sitting on the dresser. Jack had teased her about bringing it with her, but she hadn't given up on solving the mystery of what it was all about. "He's opened up as much as he can right now. He was honest about not being able to share everything. And I told him I'd be patient."

"You? Patient?" Shelly laughed. "Come on, Belle. It's eating you up and you know it. You sure you want to take on a guy with that kind of baggage? A guy who won't even *tell* you about his baggage?"

"What I'm sure of is that I need friends who support me." Her voice was sharper than she'd intended, but she was getting tired of being treated like a child who didn't know her own mind.

"I'm sorry. I'm just trying to protect you. I want you to be happy." Shelly did have a big heart. And she was Belle's oldest and best friend.

"I *am* happy. Honestly, I am. Jack is perfect for me. He likes watching old black-and-white movies with me. He doesn't mind when I play K-pop music at full volume, and I've even caught him humming along. He doesn't treat me like a baby sister or a little girl. He treats me like an equal. Like someone he really has feelings for."

"That sounds wonderful," Shelly said. "No wonder you fell in love with him. Just be sure that he loves you back and that this is what you want—life in small-town Texas, sharing a house in the suburbs with Mr. Down-to-Earth and his three-legged dog."

"It's exactly what I want, and I'm positive he loves me. As far as his secrets go, I can wait."

"Yeah…" Shelly drew out the word with skepticism. "Waiting is not your thing. Belle Fortune always has a way to get what she wants when she wants it."

"I promised I'd stop bugging him."

"You didn't promise you wouldn't figure it out on your own."

"What does *that* mean?"

"Remember back in college, when that loser tried to convince you he was British royalty?"

"Are you talking about Andrew Middlethorpe?" She ran her fingers through her hair in frustration. "Do you and my brothers keep a worksheet somewhere of all the bad dating choices I've made? I was twenty."

"We don't, but let's face it—we could," Shelly answered with a laugh. "I'm not talking about the way you fell head over heels for the supposed future duke. I'm talking about how you were clever enough to do an online search of royal peerages and discovered he not only didn't have a title, but his real name wasn't even Middlethorpe. Wasn't it Jones or something?"

It had only taken a few hours to track down a list of British royalty by rank and title to realize Andrew's family was nowhere on it. And that he didn't even exist, at least not with the name Middlethorpe.

"What's your point, Shelly?"

"My point is if you want to know more about Jack, there are ways to do it yourself."

"I don't want to check up on the man I love. I know who he is, for crying out loud. His sister is married to my cousin."

"Okay, fine. All I'm saying is—if you don't want to pressure him for details, you have other options to get the info you want." Shelly pressed her case. "You'd be doing him a favor, really. You know, by not making him talk about it."

After they said goodbye, Belle thought about what Shelly suggested. There probably *was* a database somewhere of soldiers who won military medals. She could read up on what he did to earn the medal. He'd said he didn't want to *talk* about it. He never specifically said he didn't want her to *know* about it. Maybe a little research on her part really would be doing Jack a favor.

Chapter Thirteen

Jack pulled into his sister's drive and noticed Brady's truck was gone. Not all that unusual, but Harper had asked him to come help her with a carpentry project in the attic, so he assumed Brady would be around as well. He grabbed his toolbox from the back of the truck and headed in.

"Hey, Jack!" Harper threw her arms around his neck in the doorway. "How *are* you?"

"Uh…fine." Why was she acting like they hadn't seen each other in weeks?

She caught his expression and bit her lip for a second. "Okay, look—you and I haven't had a brother-sister sit-down in a while, and I thought we needed one."

"Are you telling me there are no shelves to put up?" God save him from curious women. First Belle and now his sister.

"I really do need shelves. Brady took the boys and the baby over to visit Arabella and Jay so we could have some private time." She turned and led him to the stairs going up to the attic.

"Harper, I don't want…" She turned on the steps and gave that you-will-do-what-I-tell-you look that made her such a great nanny, and now a parent. He dropped his head and followed her. "Fine. But please don't grill me all day."

The so-called project was mindlessly simple. The shelves were precut and finished. It was something Brady could have handled easily. Harper started with random chitchat as he got to work— how the kids were doing, how Christina was sleeping through the night now, how well Brady was doing as concierge at the Hotel Fortune. Jack was lining the first shelf up on the wall when she finally got down to business.

"So how are things, now that Belle has moved in?"

"They're good. Really good."

"I get the feeling she's The One for you."

He couldn't help grinning a little at that. "I get the same feeling, sis."

"Have you told her you're in love with her?"

"News flash, Harper—it's the twenty-first century and grown-ups don't always need big declarations." He squeezed the trigger on the power screwdriver. "We live together. We share a bed. And we're happy. That's all that should matter to you."

She watched in silence as he screwed the shelf onto the wall, waiting until he set the power tool down.

"Your happiness *is* what matters to me. I'm just curious if you've told *her* what you won't tell me."

"And what's that?" Jack knew, of course, but he really hoped his sister wouldn't go there. Not now. Maybe not ever.

She paused. "I got a call this week from Steve Jennings."

Jack's heart leaped, then stopped completely before starting an uneven staccato in his chest. Steve had been calling Jack for a few weeks now, but he'd declined the calls. He wasn't ready for that conversation. Wasn't ready to hear how much his onetime friend hated Jack for what happened to him. It was Jack's fault that Steve had been left with only one leg. What else would the guy want to share with Jack other than rage and hurt? Which was totally justified, but… He just wasn't ready to hear it yet. No matter how much he deserved it.

Harper's voice was gentle. "Steve said he's been trying to reach you and you aren't returning his calls. Then he remembered you'd given him my number as a contact, just in case…" Her words trailed off. In case Jack had died. The guys in the unit did that—traded next-of-kin numbers so someone who'd actually known them would be able to speak to their families if something happened.

And something *had* happened. But Jack had come through it unscathed.

"What did he say to you?" Steve wasn't the kind of guy to take his anger out on an innocent bystander, but he'd gone through the trouble to call Harper, so who knew what he'd been feeling?

"What's that tone about?" Harper leaned forward. "Jack, he said he really needs to talk to you. He's worried about you. He said to tell you he's doing great."

That was a lie. How could he be doing great after the mistakes Jack had made?

Harper continued, "He said to tell you to—and I'm quoting here—'get your head out of your butt and call him.'" Jack was staring at the floor, so Harper had to lower her head and look up to get his attention. "What's going on? Why does the guy you told me several times over the past few years was your best friend think you have your head up your butt? Why are you not speaking to him? What happened?"

He ground his teeth together so tightly he was surprised he didn't hear them cracking. "Harper, I'm not some high school kid anymore. I don't owe you explanations."

She sat back and her shoulders fell.

"You're right. You don't owe me anything. But I didn't stop caring about you the day you turned eighteen. I worried about you every day when you were overseas." Her voice grew stronger, and she leaned forward again, shaking her finger at his face. "And now I see you building a new life with an amazing young woman, and you're going to blow it all to hell. Secrets always come out—usually in the most painful ways. I know you better than anyone, Jack Radcliffe. I know there's something wrong. If you won't tell Belle, then tell *me*. Not because you owe it to me, but because you owe it to yourself."

"Stop!" Jack barked out the word, and it echoed back at him in the small attic. He scrubbed his hands down his face. His voice dropped to a plea. "Please stop. I'm doing you a favor by not telling you."

"Don't pull that high-and-mighty hero routine on me. Just because you won medals—"

"I didn't want that damn medal. I didn't deserve it."

"Tell me why you feel that way, Jack." It was the sudden softness in his sister's voice that finally broke him.

"I got three good men killed, that's why." His voice was leaden. "My best friend lost his leg. Because of me. I'm no hero, Harper. I'm a fool."

The attic was warm and silent. Outside, he could hear cars driving by. Rain coming down on the roof. A gust of wind once in a while. But inside, nothing made a sound, other than his own heart pounding blood through his veins. Drumming in his ears. Harper stared at him with wide eyes, not saying a word. Waiting. She was right. It had to come out sooner or later.

"Things were pretty quiet when the last deployment started." He was surprised how level his own voice was. "One of those weird lulls in the Middle East where you started to feel like peace might actually be taking hold. We were providing training and support for the Iraqi troops, and we developed a relationship with a village not far from the base. Kinda took them under our wing, you know?" He swallowed hard, not expecting her to answer. "Drilled a well so they could get water more easily. Repaired buildings damaged during earlier skirmishes. They were good people—families who'd lived in that area for generations, living their lives and trying to avoid being dragged into the wars that kept washing over their little valley." He paused, remembering the smell of herbs drying in the window of Khalid's home. The sound of children playing soccer with the equipment Jack's friends had donated. "I became friends with the leader of the village…Khalid. We got permission from him and from our command to help build a school for the girls in the village, so they could get the same education their brothers were getting. It was a humanitarian mission."

Harper's voice was thick with emotion. "Mom would have been so proud of that, Jack." Their mother had been an elementary school teacher. "You did a good thing."

"We were just getting started when the local militias got wind of what we were doing. We got as far as laying the foundation before they stopped us." His eyes fell closed. All he could smell now was dust and blood. All he could hear was artillery fire and screams.

"They ambushed us up in the hills. One minute we were driving along, arguing about the best way to construct the school's roof, the next minute our vehicle was upside-down and taking fire. The supply truck behind us was in flames." He pulled in a breath, seeing the scene unwind against his eyelids like the disaster that it was. "There'd been no sign of enemy activity on that road. We had no warning."

"Oh, Jack. You can't blame yourself." Harper's logic was so naive. His eyes snapped open in fury.

"The school was *my* idea. I recruited *my* friends to volunteer to help me. I put us all there." Jack swallowed hard. "Steve and I crawled out of our vehicle and were pinned down by sniper fire right away. He was hit in the leg. I returned fire and dragged him behind some rocks. Got a few others to cover and called for reinforcements. There was a drone nearby and it scattered the rebels pretty fast. It was over in maybe…ten or fifteen minutes." His head dropped. "Fifteen minutes to end three lives and ruin a few more. Steve lost a leg. Jerry lost the sight in one eye. Greg had his arm broken in three places. He was a musician…"

"And you?" Harper's voice was almost a whisper, raw with emotion.

"A few bruises and sprains. Roughed up my shoulder." He looked up at her. "I could have made it to your wedding, you know. The attack was in October. My discharge was in December."

"You said you didn't get out until Jan—" Her eyes went soft and shiny with tears. "Oh, I see. You lied to me." She raised her hand before he could speak. "I understand, Jack. To go right from…what you went through…to a wedding…"

"To *five* weddings. At once."

Harper cringed. "I get it. I can see why you would have felt overwhelmed. Still, Jack. I'm your sister. You could have told me the truth."

Jack rolled his eyes. "Seriously? Not only were you getting married, you were also eight months pregnant. I was supposed to ruin that by telling you I was responsible for an incident that killed three people?"

She wiped a tear from her cheek and blinked away a few more. Her face was pale. "If you were responsible, why did they give you a medal?"

He went still. "I wish to hell I'd never told you that."

"Was that another lie?" There was no anger in her question.

"No. But it was ridiculous."

"I never thought of the Army as a group that hands out ridiculous medals. There must have been a reason." Harper was always so practical.

"One of the guys put me in for it, I guess. Probably Jerry—he was only eighteen and he had a bit of hero worship. Painted me as some superhuman who saved lives instead of losing them."

"But you said you dragged them to safety. You shot at the attackers. Sounds pretty heroic to me."

He shook his head. "I led them into the ambush in the first place."

Harper didn't answer. Jack turned and finished putting up the shelves without any further conversation. In fact, they didn't speak again until they were back downstairs, where Harper made a pot of coffee. He could tell she had more to say, but she waited until they were both seated with coffee in front of them.

"You need to tell Belle what happened." Before he could object, she added, "And you should probably talk to a professional, too."

"No, thanks to both suggestions."

"Jack, you and Belle love each other."

He straightened. "Did she tell you that?"

"Please. I have eyes. I know what love looks like."

He jammed his fingers through his hair. He knew he loved Belle. He just didn't know if he should. How could they possibly last long-term?

"We're so different, Harper. She showed me pictures on her phone last night of the house she grew up in, and it's a freakin' mansion. Her favorite hobby is shopping. Sure, we're having fun right now, but long-term? I can't possibly give her the lifestyle she's used to, and she'll realize it eventually. I'm sure as hell no Fortune."

Harper sipped her coffee thoughtfully. "Not all

Fortunes are rich—look at Brady. But I'll admit, the Fortune family can be a lot to handle, even the ones of modest means. Especially for folks like us who came from smaller, more laid-back families. You've seen how chaotic a small cookout can be, and that's nothing compared to a big holiday dinner." She chuckled at some memory. "It's not always easy to love a Fortune—especially for introverts like us. But I can tell you it is always worth it."

"I don't know, sis." He shook his head. "Belle's looking for a Prince Charming, not some Dark Knight."

She grabbed his hand and squeezed it. "Your heart has never been dark. Something bad happened, and you need to deal with it. Sooner rather than later. And you also need to sit down and talk to Belle. Secrets are no good for a relationship."

He didn't answer. Everyone kept pressuring him to talk, talk, talk. But he'd just told Harper everything and he did *not* feel better for it. He felt bad for putting that story in her head. Speaking the story out loud brought up feelings inside of him that were the opposite of feeling better. There was no way he could tell Belle what happened. She'd lived a pampered life, and who knows what she'd think of the story not only of death, but of his own failure?

Harper reached out and put her hand over his. He looked at her, and surprisingly did not find horror or disappointment in her eyes. Only tenderness.

"Do you remember what I told you about how Brady and I met?"

"You were his twins' nanny, right?"

She nodded. "And do you remember me telling you how badly I messed things up?" He frowned. It was something about the family who'd employed her before she met Brady. She filled in the blanks for him. "I kept something secret from Brady, because I thought he'd think less of me. I felt guilty about things, even though I hadn't done anything wrong. The longer I held the story in, the worse it got. Then I met the other Fortunes and I was not only worried about what Brady would think, I was worried that they'd think less of me. That I'd embarrass Brady. That his family would believe all the vile rumors that woman was spreading."

It came back to him now. Harper's former employers' marriage was on the rocks when they'd hired her to care for their children. The husband had come on to Harper, and she'd done her best to avoid being anywhere near him. Then the guy left his wife, and the wife blamed Harper, insisting that she'd had an affair with her husband—which had never happened.

"I was a wreck inside, Jack." She slumped in

her chair. "I was sure every day was going to be the day that story got out, and Brady and his whole family would shun me or something."

"That's a little drastic, don't you think?"

"In hindsight?" she answered. "Sure. But keeping it inside made it feel bigger and scarier. Then that horrid woman made a scene at the Easter brunch, and I thought I'd die of humiliation. I figured Brady and I were done." She smiled wistfully. "But Brady stood by me and didn't believe her lies. And the Fortunes all stood by me, too." She paused. "My point is…the longer you wait, the more you'll convince yourself of the worst-case scenario. Belle's no fragile flower, Jack. I don't think there's any such thing in the Fortune family. She can take it."

Maybe Belle could handle it. But if not, having her walk away right now was something he didn't think he could take.

Chapter Fourteen

Belle cleaned the kitchen after Jack made breakfast. A leisurely Sunday breakfast was becoming part of their routine. They'd talk about the previous week and what was coming up the next week, and catch up with each other's lives.

Last Sunday, they'd spent the time jotting down ideas for the charitable foundation he'd been talking about starting. Pairing hard-to-place rescue animals with veterans was a project that could save both the animal and the veteran. He'd been enthusiastic about the plans.

But Jack had been quiet today. Almost sullen. Definitely withdrawn. The mood had started after his visit to Harper's yesterday. Maybe they'd argued, but about what? Maybe about whatever he was refusing to discuss. Whatever gave him those bad dreams. He'd made it clear he didn't want to talk about it, but Belle didn't even know what "it" was. And that bothered her. He was outside now, trimming some of the overgrown hedges out front. She finished drying the omelet pan and put it away.

Was it something from his childhood? Something about losing his parents? About his military service? Did he have some horrible dark secret, or was he holding her at arm's length for some other reason? Was he trying to avoid getting too deep? Too close? Had they moved too fast? Was he getting cold feet?

She tossed the towel in the sink in frustration. She didn't like the unknown. Never had. Maybe it had something to do with being the youngest of seven. She'd hated it when her older siblings shut her out of conversations because she was "too young." Usually she'd figured out a way to find out what was going on—either by pushing her way into the conversation or by doing a little detective work. Because not knowing bugged her. Knowing that Jack was intentionally keeping her out of some part of his life bugged her even more.

It was *still* bugging her the next afternoon at work. Belle chewed her lower lip as she stared at the computer screen. This particular online search had nothing to do with investments. Taking Shelly's advice, she'd decided to take matters into her own hands. She'd agreed not to pressure Jack but that didn't mean she couldn't find out what he was hiding. For her own peace of mind.

She'd ended up going down a frustrating rabbit hole of military record searches and national archives requests, and she still hadn't found what she wanted. His service was too recent to show up in any of the military archives yet, and she had no idea what kind of medal he'd received. She'd tried plugging his name into her normal internet search engine, but nothing unusual came up.

She was chewing the tip of her pen when the desk phone rang, making her jump. She transferred the call to Beau, then leaned toward the screen again. She knew getting closer didn't make it more likely she'd see what she wanted, but—

"Everything okay out here?" Beau's voice behind her made her jump. She quickly minimized the screen, then turned in the chair with her brightest smile.

"Fine! Great! At least until the moment my brother gave me a heart attack." She winked, doing her best to look playful and composed.

"Really? Is that why you took Mr. Powell's call and put it through to *me*, even though he asked for

Draper and has always been Draper's client?" Beau sat on the edge of her desk and folded his arms on his chest. "What are you doing that has you so mesmerized?" He leaned over and looked at her screen. "A spreadsheet? No way. Even you don't get drawn *that* deep into a profit and loss report. What's going on?"

She could deny it, but that wasn't how things worked in her family. They were honest with each other.

"I'm sorry, Beau. I'm thinking about Jack and me and how things are going."

"Trouble in paradise? Draper tried to tell you not to move in with the guy so fast."

"It was fast. I think part of it was I was so tired of living out of a hotel room."

"We invited you to move in with us."

"In your bachelor pad?" She grimaced, making Beau laugh. "No, thanks."

"Things seemed pretty tight between you and Jack," Beau answered. "What happened?"

She sighed. "I think I got ahead of myself and freaked him out."

"Aw, sis. You charge into every relationship thinking it will be forever. And then you end up getting hurt."

"It's not like that. I love him, Beau. I *really* love him. And I want him to love me back. Right now.

And to share everything with me. Right now." Her nose wrinkled. "I just… There's something he says he's not ready to share with me yet, but…"

"But, being Belle Fortune, as soon as someone says you can't have something, the more you're determined to get it. You're like a velvet bulldozer—sugar and spice and get-out-of-your-way."

She laughed, but the truth of his comment pinched her heart. "Does that make me a bad person?"

His smile vanished, and he pulled her up from the chair and into a brotherly hug. "Absolutely not! It makes you a clever problem solver, and you always lead with your heart." He held her out at arm's length. "If Jack Radcliffe doesn't see that… well, that's his loss. But just to play devil's advocate here." He lowered his head to look straight into her eyes. "He may have a reason for not telling you whatever it is that you're so desperate to know. Be careful what you go after, kiddo. It might just blow up all over you like that glitter bomb you sent me as a joke for my twenty-first birthday. I ended up joining my college debate team in a major competition with sparkly hair. That stuff really stuck."

She remembered Beau's furious call that afternoon years ago. It was meant as a gag gift—she'd had no idea he'd open the package right before a debate competition. Just like she had no idea what she was going to find out about Jack if she kept searching. But she couldn't stop now.

It took another two hours before she hit pay dirt. After giving up on the military searches, she'd gone back to an old-fashioned internet search. His name hadn't worked, so she decided to delve into news stories about Fort Drum in northern New York. Maybe whatever happened would have made the paper. And sadly, it did.

Three Fort Drum Soldiers Die in Ambush

Jack's name wasn't mentioned, but she knew this was what she was looking for. Three men's faces looked back at her from the screen. All three were dead. And one of them was Corporal James Whitney. Jack had screamed the name *Jimmy* in his sleep a few weeks ago. She read the sparse details over and over. A group of soldiers on a humanitarian mission. An ambush in the mountains. Four survivors.

Belle had no way to even imagine what that must have been like. Gunfire. Explosions. Dying men… People Jack knew. Men he was probably in charge of. No wonder he didn't want to talk about it. But *shouldn't* he? To someone? The Army must provide help to men who'd been through a battle like that.

She did more digging. There was a veterans' hospital and clinic in Austin, only an hour or so away. And they had counseling services and group sessions. She printed a few pages of details and contact information, along with a couple articles on veterans and PTSD. Ready or not, Jack needed to talk to someone.

She didn't mention it until after dinner, when she and Jack followed Sarge outside to watch the sunset. She carried out a bottle of wine and two glasses. He watched in silence as she poured it and slid a glass his way. Dinner had been quiet for both of them, and he raised an eyebrow at her as he lifted his glass.

"What's up, Belle? You look like you have something to say."

She blew out a breath. "I know you've asked me to be patient about—"

Jack's eyes closed. "Please don't do this."

"Hear me out." She put her hand over his. He didn't respond. "I'm not going to ask you to tell me about it." He looked up in surprise, and she took it as a good sign. "Because I already know."

"You *what*?" He yanked his hand away from hers, sitting bolt upright in his seat. "Did Harper tell you?"

She blinked. He'd told his sister and not her. Belle raised her chin and held her voice steady. "No, she didn't. But I'm glad you were able to talk to her." She tried to hold the next words in, but couldn't. "Even if you couldn't tell *me*."

He paused, his eyes narrowing. "What is it you think you know? Or is this a fishing expedition?"

She bristled. "It's not a fishing expedition. You were involved in an ambush that left three other men dead, right?"

Jack went very still. "How could you possibly…?"

"It doesn't matter." His anger had her rethinking her strategy. He wouldn't be amused to learn she'd been searching the internet for news on him.

"The hell it doesn't." His chair clattered across the flagstones as he pushed to his feet, glaring down at her. A rush of defensive anger propelled her to her feet, too. She spread her hands wide.

"I did some online digging, okay? It was in the newspaper from Fort Drum, and even though your name wasn't mentioned, the timing seemed right." Her voice lowered. "Why are you so angry? You said you couldn't tell me, and now you don't have to. The elephant is in the room and we can *both* see it and deal with it. Together."

His mouth fell open, then he clamped it shut and tipped his head back, staring up at the blue-gray sky above them. She could almost hear him counting to ten in his head before he ground out the next words.

"You did an internet search about something

I told you I didn't want to talk about? You researched me like some portfolio for the family business?"

She didn't like the way he said *family business*. "First, *you're* the one who held something back in this relationship. You said you didn't want to talk about it, not that I couldn't go find out on my own." She shushed the voice in the back of her mind telling her that was a flimsy argument. "And second, what does my family have to do with this?"

"I don't know." He rubbed the back of his neck. "It seems the Fortunes are used to getting what they want, one way or the other."

"That's not fair…" Her voice trailed off.

For a few seconds he said nothing, then, "Look, you're right. This is between you and me. But I told you I didn't want what happened overseas coming between us."

"It's *already* come between us. And honestly, Jack, now you don't have to tell me about it. It's out there, and we can deal with it. My dad always says you can't solve a problem you can't define. Now I know. You clearly have survivor's guilt." She'd read about that on the VA website. "I get it. We can work on that."

Jack stared at Belle in disbelief.

"We can work on it? How is that going to happen, exactly? Are you going to bring three men back to life?" His voice rose with each word, and Sarge hopped his way back up to the patio to look between them with concern. "You think you know what happened because you read some sanitized news story? Trust me—you don't."

"Then *tell* me, Jack. Tell me what I'm missing. Because if it's worse than what I read, then you need to talk to someone. If not me, then someone." She pointed at him. "And don't tell me you can't talk about it, because you obviously told Harper."

"So...the problem is you're jealous?" Tension was buzzing under his skin. Anger. Panic.

She threw her arms in the air. "Oh, for God's sake! I'm not jealous of your sister. What are we even arguing about right now?" She stepped toward him, but he pulled back. He saw the pain in her eyes when he did. This whole scene felt... For lack of a better word, it felt like an ambush.

"You suckered me in with a nice dinner and the wine and the sunset." He glowered at her, knowing he wasn't being completely reasonable. "Then you tell me, all proud of yourself, that you figured out my secret like that was something I wanted you to do. I didn't tell you for a reason."

"And what exactly was that reason?" She was standing rigid in front of him, beautiful and dangerous. "By the way, if you think a nice meal is some evil plot, then what the heck are we even doing? If you don't know me better than that…"

He turned away, not knowing what to do. What to say. They were both angry. And anger made people say stupid things. Things that took a second to say, but could leave scars for a long time. Not watching her made it easier to speak, so he spoke to the wall.

"You only know a piece of what happened. I still don't want to talk about it. That's my right, Belle. I know you're used to getting your way, but you can't bulldoze me on this one." He turned back to face her. "If you really need me to dot the *i*'s and cross the *t*'s—if I didn't make it clear enough before—then I'll do that now. I do *not* want to talk about that day with you. Ever. If you can't respect my wishes on that, then maybe we need to rethink this whole thing."

Her face fell. "What do you— Rethink what?"

"Rethink us, Belle. This." He gestured at the space between them. "It was never going to be anything long-term anyway, so maybe this is a good point to just…stop."

She blinked a few times, her face turning ashen. "Are you breaking up with me? Because I did one thing you're not happy about?"

"Well, look at us. We're both ticked off. You can't undo what you did. You told me you did it so I wouldn't have to talk about it, but we've done nothing *but* talk about it. You're already looking at me differently." He steeled himself against the tears pooling in her eyes. "You think I'm damaged now. You want to fix me, but I don't need that. I don't want that." He could feel his soul retreating behind his defenses. "I don't deserve that, Belle."

He didn't deserve *her*.

"Jack..." His name came out like a breath. She rested her hand on her stomach, as if holding herself together. "Don't do this. Being angry doesn't mean we have to end things. You don't throw away a chance at love because you're mad about something. You stay and fight. We can work through this."

"How?" He rolled his eyes, frustrated that she seemed to be willfully clueless right now. "You're not going to give up and accept how I feel about this. It's not in your nature." He felt matching tides of panic and resolve rising inside of him. "Look, you don't have to leave tonight. It's late. I'll sleep on the couch. But come on—we knew it would come to this eventually."

"You keep saying that, and I have no freaking clue what you're talking about!" Her brows lowered into a glare. "Is there some magical expiration date on us that I didn't know about?"

He stared up at the sky again and drew in a slow

breath. He wound his fingers together on the top of his head and thought for a moment. Just because the inevitable was happening sooner than he'd expected didn't mean it had to be ugly. He looked at her, gutted to see tears on her cheeks.

"Look…it's been fun. More than fun. It's been terrific. You helped me make the transition from hell back to real life again. But you and I weren't written in the stars or anything. We come from completely different worlds. You're a princess raised in a lifestyle I'll never know. I'm an ex-soldier who pounds nails for a living."

The remaining color drained from her face, and she swayed a little on her feet. Her voice was raspy with emotion. "So you thought all along that we were just a fling?"

A drumbeat got louder and louder in his head, telling him on one beat that he was making a terrible mistake, and on the next beat that he was doing what needed to be done.

"More than a fling, Belle. But you want a guy who talks about his feelings and can whisk you off to some exotic getaway whenever the mood strikes."

She stepped forward, spots of angry color rising on her pale cheeks. "What I want is *you*, Jack. All of you—warts and all. I love you. And I know you love me. You won't admit it, not even to yourself. You're punishing yourself for whatever happened. Punishing *me* for caring. That won't stop me from loving you."

"Don't."

"You can't stop me." Her chin rose again. There was a moment of silence between them, heavy with unspoken emotion. All he had to do was open his arms and she'd be in them. His pain would ease. If there was any hope for him to find happiness, it might be with this stubborn blonde. But why should he get to have hope?

"I think we need to stop before either one of us gets any deeper in." He was already drowning.

Her eyes narrowed, and she gave a jerking nod before walking into the house. He carried the wine and glasses into the kitchen, then minutes later he heard her coming down the hall. She was pulling a suitcase behind her.

"I said you didn't have to go—"

"There's no point in staying. I called the Hotel Fortune and got a room." Her voice sounded brittle. "I'll come back for the rest of my things while you're at work."

"What happened to me not being able to stop you from loving me?" The fact that she'd folded this quickly had to mean she'd never meant a word of it.

She stopped near the door to the garage, going

to one knee to pet Sarge, who was whining softly at her feet. The dog could sense something was breaking. That something was Jack's heart. And he felt powerless to stop it.

Belle looked over her shoulder at him when she stood and reached for the door. "I love you, but that doesn't mean I'm going to let you hurt me any more than you already have."

He was the one who told her to go. Yet somehow he never imagined she really would.

"You're leaving."

"Of course I'm leaving. You've declared that we're through."

"Well…yeah, but—" She was right, but seeing her at the door with her suitcase was tearing him up inside. He'd started this, but seeing the reality of it was too much to bear. Maybe there was time to dial it back. "Is all of this because I don't want to talk about the worst day of my life?"

"No, Jack. We could have figured that out. But if you never had any real hope for us in the first place…if you won't even admit to yourself that you love me…if you have to use some BS excuse about me being a Fortune as if that somehow makes me unlovable—" Her voice broke.

"That's not what I said." What was happening? He had to stop her. She swallowed hard.

"I've dealt with the guys who only wanted me

because of my name. But this? You using my name as a reason why you *don't* want me? That hurts more."

And she was gone. Leaving that last sentence hanging in the air to slowly choke him. He'd hurt her. He turned away, his hands curling into fists. This pain? This was exactly what he deserved for thinking he could have a chance at a life with a woman like Belle. He'd never meant to hurt her, but it was better they end it now, before he could hurt her even worse. He poured himself a glass of whiskey, knowing wine wasn't going to do the trick tonight.

Chapter Fifteen

"He broke up with you because you're a Fortune?" Meg shook her head over their morning coffee at Kirby's Perks. "Obviously, I'm biased... but that makes no sense."

It had been three days since Belle walked out of Jack's house with the last of her things. It was the hardest thing she'd ever done, but she respected herself too much to stay.

"That was just an excuse." She sipped her coffee but couldn't taste it. Probably because she'd barely slept since that night. "There was more to it than that. I..." She hesitated. It wasn't her place to talk about the ambush in Iraq. "I overstepped

my bounds. Pressured him to talk about something he didn't want to talk about. You know how
it is—a cornered animal will lash out, and that's
what he did."

"But he ended *everything* over that? That seems
extreme."

"It was a heat-of-the-moment thing."

Meg set her coffee cup down and stared hard
at Belle. "Why are you defending him? The guy
dumped you."

"Technically, I walked out."

"Stop it." Meg reached for Belle's hand. "You
didn't leave until he told you it was over. Stop
framing this to be your fault."

One minute Belle was calm and clear-eyed. The
next her cheeks were wet with tears. She dug into
her bag, searching for tissues. "It may not have
been my fault, but I'm not exactly innocent. He
asked me not to do something and I did it anyway.
I told myself I was doing it for his own good, but…
Jack was right. I was being stubborn." She pulled
a handful of tissues from her bag and wiped her
face, giving Meg her best attempt at a smile. "I
tend to be that way. Not my finest trait."

"I disagree. If you thought you were helping
him, then you did it out of love. And he should
have seen that."

"It's…complicated. We probably could have

gotten past that with some time, but he just quit. He didn't believe in us as much as I did."

"You still love him."

Another watery smile. "I don't know how to *stop* loving him." Belle took a deep breath and glanced at her watch. "And now I need to go to the office and try to convince my brothers not to beat up Jack or whatever it is big brothers want to do when they see their baby sister cry. They've been hovering over me nonstop."

Jack hadn't been there when she'd collected the rest of her stuff yesterday. Sarge had followed her around the house as if he knew she was leaving for good. In the end, she didn't have the heart to take the last of the shoes from the dog's closet stash. She could sacrifice one pair for Sarge.

She'd left a parting gift for Jack on their—his— bed. She'd scattered the pages she'd printed from the VA website across the bedspread. Sure, she could have left them neatly stacked on the kitchen table, but she'd had a petty impulse at the last minute and just tossed them on the bed. Maybe he'd get the hint. It was out of her hands now.

The day was quiet at the office. She had a feeling Beau and Draper were keeping it that way on purpose. It was unusual that multiple clients "asked" to reschedule their appointments that week. She could be annoyed with her brothers, but she actually appreciated the break. She was not in the mood to be dealing with people and pretending to be jolly.

Jack had hurt her, but she'd hurt him, too. Looking back on it, she understood why he felt betrayed by what she'd done. The more she'd read on PTSD and battle trauma this week—and she'd read a lot—the more she understood why he was protecting himself from reliving that day. If only she'd read that information *before* barging headlong into telling him that she knew about the incident, as if that magically made everything better. Her oldest brother, Austin, used to tell her she was a Pollyanna. A daydreamer. A bright-eyed optimist. Austin had learned a hard lesson with his first marriage. He'd trusted a woman who'd taken advantage of him and nearly ruined his reputation. But, to be fair, since then, Austin *had* found true love with his new wife, Felicity.

And so had Belle. She loved Jack, and she was sure he loved her, too. He was just too scared to admit it. Instead of pushing him again, she was going to have to do something she wasn't very good at.

She was going to have to be patient.

"If you don't stop barking at the crew doing the finish work, they're gonna walk out." Marcus came up behind Jack and put his hand on Jack's shoulder. "And you're going to be installing that crown molding yourself."

Jack grimaced. "If they can't do it right, then I might *have* to do it myself. What the hell is wrong with these guys?" He'd about had it with the crew. And the job. And the human race in general.

Marcus shook his head. "Look, I'm supposed to be the bad cop on this job site. You're the nice guy, remember? I'm too old to change my stripes and start being all kind and encouraging." He tipped his head toward the room where the crew had worked that afternoon. "They measured the first few sections wrong this morning because I left the wrong blueprint sketches in the kitchen. I don't make a lot of mistakes, but I made one today."

"Oh." Jack swallowed hard.

"Yeah. *Oh*." Marcus gave him a hard look. "You need to get that girl back in your life fast, man. You can't keep operating on whiskey and no sleep. And trust me, I speak from experience when I say that. You're spiraling, and it's not going to end well if you don't change course."

"She walked out on me, Marcus."

"You told me two days ago that you *told* her to go." Jack was losing track of what he had and hadn't told his friend.

"Doesn't matter. We were doomed anyway."

"Wow." Marcus started folding up the blueprints. "You are one massive puddle of self-pity right now, aren't you? Did you ever think that maybe the real problem is your inability to deal with your last deployment?"

Jack swore under his breath. "I am dealing with it."

Marcus leaned forward and sniffed, as if checking Jack's breath. "You're drowning it."

Jack pulled back. "I don't drink on the job, and you know it."

Marcus's expression grew somber. "No, but you're drinkin' at night. I can see it in your bloodshot eyes. You gotta reach out to the VA, man. It's not a weakness to ask for help, and they've got the right tools for you."

Jack's teeth ground together. The pages Belle had scattered on the bed when she got the last of her things were still there. He couldn't bear to get into that bed without her, so he'd been sleeping on the sofa with Sarge on the floor at his side. Sarge was as bereft at her loss as Jack.

But he knew what those pages were about. He'd seen the *Treating PTSD* headlines. *And Surviving Survivor's Guilt.* At first he'd been furious. But there was a possibility that she'd done it because she *loved* him. Because she believed they had a future. Was her belief enough to make it true?

Marcus gently kicked Jack off the job site for the rest of the day, telling him he needed to get his head on straight. And get some sleep while he was at it. Sarge was thrilled to see him, but kept looking past him to see if anyone else was coming home. Someone like Belle.

"Sorry, buddy," Jack told the dog. "Looks like I screwed up things for both of us."

It was a warm afternoon, so he sat on one of the veranda chairs and watched as Sarge slowly checked out the perimeter of the yard. Thinking of Marcus's warning, he'd grabbed a soda from the fridge instead of a beer. Normally Sarge's stubby tail was wagging the whole time he did his perimeter search, but he was half-hearted about it today. As if he was too sad to care. *Same, dog. Same.*

His phone buzzed in his pocket, and for some irrational reason, he thought it might be Belle. He didn't even look at the screen, just swiped it and tried not to sound breathless with hope.

"Belle?"

A painfully familiar male voice laughed on the other end of the call.

"It's about damn time you answered your phone, Radcliffe. And who the hell is Belle? Sounds like the princess in one of my daughter's Disney movies."

Steve Jennings. The last person in the world he

wanted to talk to. And also his best friend. It was bad enough that Jack had been avoiding answering Steve's calls. He couldn't hang up on the guy.

"Steve…hi."

Brilliant, Jack.

"I see your conversation skills have gotten rusty since Iraq." Steve sounded exactly the way he always had. Same sarcasm. Same undercurrent of easy laughter under every word. "Did you have a vocal cord injury I don't know about?"

"Uh…no."

"A hearing problem?"

"No."

"Well, then, I hate to sound like a middle school girl, but why aren't you taking my calls, Cliffie?"

Jack's mouth curved into a rueful grin at the nickname that only Steve could get away with.

"Um…" He shook his head, frustrated at his inability to form a sentence. "I'm sorry, man. I just… I didn't think I was ready to deal with…" *Nice, Jack.* "I mean, to have this conversation."

"O-kay. What exactly do you see 'this conversation' being about?"

"I don't know." *About how I cost you your leg?* "How…how are you doing?"

"I'm good. Been home for over a month now, and still getting PT a few times a week. You should see the high-tech prosthetic they've got me using.

I feel like Iron Man trying to learn how to use this thing." He chuckled. "It's not always pretty, but little Avery took me to his class as his show-and-tell exhibit so I could demonstrate how it works."

Jack couldn't get over how normal Steve sounded. No tone of resentment. No grieving. It was as if the guy who'd lost his leg had done what Jack couldn't—he'd moved on. When he stayed silent, Steve continued, "So tell me how you're doing. Your sister said you were working construction? And seriously, who's Belle? Did you find yourself a Texas princess already?"

"She's a New Orleans princess, actually." A stab of pain hit his chest. He'd answered as if Belle was still in his life. "But it's over."

"And whose idea was that?" Steve asked.

"Mine, I guess. I said some things that hurt her. She told me she deserved better. She was right. End of story." She deserved everything he couldn't give her. The lifestyle. The happiness.

"Let me give you a piece of unsolicited advice from an old married dude," Steve replied. "If the problem was created by words, it can always be solved with more—and better—words. Apologize. And mean it. That is, assuming you want her back?"

"I do." The conviction behind those two words surprised him, but only for a minute. Of course he wanted her back. That didn't mean it was going to happen.

"Then go fix it, man." Steve's voice was firm. "But first, I need to know why you're avoiding my calls. I talked to Jerry and he said you haven't returned his calls either. We all served side by side for over a year, and you vanished into thin air after you mustered out. I want to know why."

Sarge had come back to the veranda, dropping a tennis ball at Jack's feet. He bent down and tossed it for the dog to chase. Steve wasn't going to fill the silence this time. Jack blew out a long sigh.

"Why would you *want* me to call? After everything…why haven't you guys written me off?"

"Because you're my friend. Why do you think that changed?"

He blinked a few times, tossing the ball again for Sarge.

"The ambush…I led us right into it. It was my—"

"Don't you dare say that attack was your fault." There was no hint of laughter under Steve's words now. They were hard and angry. Steve rarely got angry over anything.

"What else *can* I say? That school was my idea. I dragged you guys into it."

"We knew the risks. You asked us to volunteer

and we did. It's not like you ordered us into an enemy compound unarmed."

"I may as well have. It had the same effect."

"Wow, dude. No wonder you haven't wanted to talk to anyone. You're afraid to shed that mantle of guilt you've draped over your shoulders."

Jack bristled. "What is that supposed to mean?"

"You've made that day all about you. As if you had any way of knowing we'd be ambushed. We'd had no intel on enemy forces in the area. None of the patrols had spotted any activity on that road." Steve paused. "So how exactly were *you* supposed to be the all-wise, all-knowing one who could have predicted an ambush? Get over yourself, Jack. We got blindsided. It happens."

Jack wished he'd grabbed a beer after all. The memories washed over him as if he was having a nightmare while wide-awake. The dust in his nostrils. The deafening explosions. The noxious smell of blood and sweat. A chill made him shudder. Sarge immediately lay down across Jack's feet, as if he knew his master needed the contact.

"We lost three good men." Jack's voice was hard.

"We did," Steve answered. "They were great guys. They should be alive right now, but that's not on you, pal. And let me tell you something… I'm sitting here watching my children playing in the backyard as we speak. My gorgeous wife is cooking her famous short ribs in the kitchen, humming our wedding song to herself." Steve cleared his throat. "If you want to take credit for something, take credit for *that*, Jack. You're the reason I made it home to them."

"I'm the reason you lost your leg." He didn't make his argument as firmly as he had before. It was just automatic. A mantra he'd told himself over and over since their return.

"An enemy sniper is the reason I lost my leg." There was nothing automatic in Steve's reply. His voice was firm and determined. "I'd have lost my *life* if you hadn't dragged me behind those rocks and returned fire." There was another long pause before his friend continued. "My counselor at the VA told me I was lucky, that a lot of guys have to reframe their memories of combat, because they get things all screwed up and think their version of the memory is real. I think that's what you need to do. Because you and I are remembering two different days.

"I'm remembering a day when Jack Radcliffe crawled out of a burning, overturned vehicle with his gun blazing like some guy in *Call of Duty*. You were yelling orders while laying cover for us, and those who couldn't move fast enough—like me— you grabbed us and dragged us while still firing at the enemy." Steve paused a moment. "You grabbed a radio and called in air cover at basically the same time you were doing everything else. Jack, you saved lives that day. The men we lost were gone the instant the RPGs hit us, but after that, you kept the rest of us alive."

Jack stared out across the yard, with the prairie running to the hills beyond the fence. Everything Steve said was accurate. Things had happened fast. He'd done the best he could in the chaos. In his dreams, it was nothing but a swirl of noise and panic all around him, but now he remembered having his weapon slung over his shoulder in the vehicle. He remembered swinging it forward after the crash. A lot of the noise from his memories was from *him*. He cleared his throat, almost choking on the emotion gathering there.

"I—I guess so."

"There's no guessing about it, Jack. Why do you think I recommended you for the medal in the first place?"

"That was you?"

"Me and Greg, technically. And Jerry backed up the chain of events. If you've been beating yourself up about that day…well, you need to talk to someone. That's way too much weight to carry around. It'll break you, man."

"Some days it feels like it already has."

"Get a hold of the VA and talk to someone."

"That's what people keep telling me." He rubbed the back of his neck, and for the first time, he noticed how tight the muscles were.

"People like this Belle you won't talk about?"

"Yeah." The acknowledgment came out as a breath. "She printed a bunch of stuff from the VA website, then threw them all over the bed like confetti when she left."

Steve let out a loud laugh. "I like this girl's style already. Sounds like someone you need to have in your life." His laughter faded. "I mean it, Jack. Don't try to handle this on your own. Do the work, then go get the girl. And when you get that done, plan a trip to North Carolina for a weekend. Tricia and I would love to have you. I'm doing okay. For real."

Jack huffed a soft laugh. "Sounds like you're doing better than me."

As soon as the call ended, Jack went in and grabbed up all the papers from the bed. He didn't even leave the room, just sat on the edge of the mattress and started reading. After what felt like hours, he stood and noticed Belle had left the mysterious framed rose picture on the dresser. He picked it up and studied the painted flower and its engraved frame. They never had solved the riddle of the weird rose by any other name inscription or who MAF might be.

Intentional or not, leaving the framed picture behind gave him an excuse to see her again. All he needed now was the courage.

Chapter Sixteen

Belle finished her breakfast and headed across the lobby of the Hotel Fortune for another day at work after another long, sleepless night. She hadn't seen or spoken to Jack in nearly a week. She missed him so much it made her body ache all over. Or maybe that was exhaustion. The hotel bed felt cold and empty, but at least she saw some of her family while staying there. Brady. Meg. Nicole. Ashley. All the Fortunes Jack had complained about. In a way, she could understand how the Fortunes might overwhelm an outsider. They could be a rambunctious crowd when they were together. But they were Belle's family, and she wasn't about to apologize for them.

"Belle!" She looked up to see her cousin Brian and his new bride, Emmaline, in the lobby. Emmaline was in the final trimester of her pregnancy. She sat on one of the love seats while Brian stood behind her. Emmaline waved her over.

"I swear, I can't even get from the restaurant to the elevators without sitting down to give my back a break!" Emmaline patted the cushion next to her, and Belle sat with a smile.

Brian and Emmaline were just back from a quick honeymoon stay in Austin. They were planning a bigger trip as a family after the baby was born. Emmaline leaned toward Belle.

"Hey, you got something weird on the wedding weekend, right? A picture or something?"

Belle winced. She'd left that picture at Jack's. Maybe by accident, maybe because she subconsciously wanted an excuse to go there at some point to see him. She nodded.

"Yes. A picture of a rose in a pretty frame, with a weird little quote on the back."

Brian leaned against a column near the love seat. "Well, we did a little sleuthing while we were on our honeymoon." He winked. "Emmaline called it our mystery weekend honeymoon.

She thinks it could be a thing…give couples a puzzle to solve while they're together."

"Sort of a test, to see how they work together." Emmaline smiled.

Belle arched an eyebrow high. "Isn't it a little late to find that out *after* the wedding?"

Brian laughed. "That's what *I* said. Anyway, we paid a visit to the Austin Savings Bank while we were there. Brady got that weird horse head statue before the wedding, and there was a safe-deposit key in the back of it. Then that mysterious letter gave us permission to open the box. So we did!"

"Oh," Belle said, "please tell me the box was full of diamonds and rubies!"

Emmaline shook her head. "No such luck. The note with the key said 'The Key to the Future.' But there was nothing in the safe-deposit box except a little envelope with a piece of paper inside. There was another poem on it. Do you have it, Brian?"

He was already reaching for his pocket. He pulled out a piece of paper and handed it to Belle.

What is mine is yours. What is yours is mines.
I hope you can read between the lines.
Love is forever, love never dies.
You'll see it, too, when you look in her eyes.
MAF

Belle read the typed words again out loud, then said, "This poem makes even less sense than the one on my picture. And the spelling is so weird. They were desperate for a rhyme, I guess. But the initials..." She looked up in surprise. "They're the same initials I found on the picture—*MAF*. I wonder who it is. Or was. Or maybe it stands for something? So weird."

Emmaline reached for Brian's hand so she could stand, her hand cradling her baby bump. "Right? Every time we find an answer, we end up with more questions than we had in the first place."

Maybe that was something Belle could do this week to distract herself. She could do some online searches for MAF or rose pictures or bad poetry to see if she could get any closer to solving the ever-deepening mystery.

They parted ways with a hug, and Belle went to the office. She greeted her brothers, doing her best to ignore their worried looks. She had to do a better job of pretending to be okay. She got right to work, sitting at her computer to check the daily schedule. After lunch she started filling out an on-line order form for office supplies.

"Oh, man." Draper's voice behind her was hard, startling Belle out of her inventory list. "You are definitely in the wrong place, pal."

She looked back at him, surprised at the fury she saw in his eyes. She was even more surprised to turn and see the object of that anger.

Jack was standing in the lobby.

The sight of him made her heart leap. Was he leaving town, never to see her again? Maybe he wanted to come say goodbye in a public place, to avoid a scene. Too bad her brothers hadn't gotten the *avoid a scene* memo. Beau had come out of his office, too—glaring at Jack with an expression identical to Draper's. *Oh, dear.*

"Stand down, boys." She stood and waved them off. "I love you for charging out here, but I can handle this." She turned to Jack and did her best to look composed, even though her whole body trembled at being this close to him again. "Why are you here, Jack?"

For the briefest of moments, she thought of her mother's favorite movie, and imagined Jack sweeping her off her feet and carrying her out of there like Richard Gere did with Debra Winger. Such an odd, yet crystal clear, mental image. And she wanted it so badly. *Take me back, Jack.*

He was watching her brothers, who had *not* stood down at all. In fact, Draper had moved forward toward Jack. He wasn't as tall as Jack, but she had no doubt he could hold his own in a fight. Draper's eyes narrowed.

"The door's right behind you. Feel free to use it."

Belle put her hands on her hips, hope and fear creating a wild adrenaline mix.

"I swear to God, Draper, if you don't back off, I will throw this stapler at you. And you know I won't miss. It's sweet that you're so concerned about defending my honor or whatever, but you two don't even know what happened between Jack and me."

Beau searched her eyes. "We know how sad you've been all week. Are you telling us you're still in love with this guy?"

"That's a conversation for Jack and me to have. Alone." She looked back to Jack. "If that's what he wants."

He didn't answer. His face was drawn, as if he hadn't slept any better that week than she had. Had his nightmares gotten worse? He grimaced. Was he in pain?

"Jack? Are you okay?"

His harsh laughter surprised her.

"I am the opposite of okay, and you know it more than anyone." He ran his fingers through his hair, then met her gaze. He looked confused. "I—I didn't really think this through. I didn't plan on stopping. I was coming back from Austin. From the veteran's hospital. I went to a group session this morning."

Belle moved toward him. Draper reached for her, then withdrew his hand quickly when she glared at him. She didn't have to say a word.

Draper stepped back with a bemused "Yes, ma'am."

She stopped in front of Jack, looking up at him. But he was looking past her, to her brothers. He nodded at them.

"I respect what you're both feeling right now. I screwed up, big-time. And in the process, I hurt your sister. Of all the mistakes I've made in my life—and I've made some doozies—hurting the woman I love is by far the biggest." His gaze dropped to meet hers. "I'm very glad she's got a family full of Fortunes at her back. Not only her siblings, but all those cousins, too. She deserves a family like that." His eyes searched hers while she tried to remember how to breathe. Her lungs had failed when he said *the woman I love.* The corner of his mouth lifted. "Can we talk?"

"If my Neanderthal brothers will give me the rest of the day off." She glanced back at them. Draper still looked skeptical, but Beau nodded and winked at her.

"Go for it, Belle." He grabbed her purse from her desk and tossed it at her. "And, Jack? Remember all those Fortunes are still here in Rambling Rose if you ever hurt her again."

Jack slid his arm over her shoulder, making her dizzy. *What was happening?* He grinned at

Beau and Draper before leading her out the door.
"I wouldn't want it any other way."

Jack was feeling a little light-headed having
Belle at his side again. They'd only been apart a
few days, but he'd been convinced that they were
finished. He'd even done his best to convince himself that's what he wanted. Time, and all that yap-
ping by Marcus and Steve helped him see the light.
Well, that and a scalding visit from Harper last
night, right after he'd talked to Steve and was feeling especially raw.

He'd opened the door to find his sister standing
there, her infant daughter strapped to her front in
some knot of fabric that wound around Harper. He
knew righteous indignation when he saw it, and
he was sure seeing it then. Her eyes had narrowed to slits.

"What. Have. You. Done?" She'd marched past
him.

"Gee, sis, whatever are you talking about?"

"Don't get smart with me, Jack Radcliffe." She'd
spun around, one arm steadying the baby. "Brady
told me Belle's back at the Hotel Fortune, and no-
body's happy about it, least of all her. What did
you say to her?"

"I may have said something about her family,
and our differences, and—"

"And you told her about Iraq?"

"Actually she told me. I could have handled it better."

He'd told Harper about the argument, Belle walking out, Steve's call. Then he'd showed her the VA papers that had been on his bed. She'd looked at him in disbelief.

"You are such an idiot." She'd grabbed the papers from his hands and scanned them. "Let's figure out how to fix this."

"I love you, sis."

She'd rolled her eyes. "You'd better. I'm gonna order some pizza. This may take a while."

It had taken a couple of hours, but after a few phone calls they'd found an opening in the counseling schedule, talked through all the things he specifically had to apologize to Belle for, and then Harper had insisted he get a good night's sleep in his own bed, not the sofa. His sister had helped him make sense of everything. Of course, she'd also told him to wait a few days before contacting Belle, but that particular piece of advice didn't stick. On the way home from Austin today, after an exhausting but enlightening hour of group therapy with other veterans, he'd felt the tide turning. He had to see her.

And now she was walking out to his truck with him. With a weird grin on her face.

"What's that smile about?"

She started to giggle. "When you walked in there, I had this wacky vision of that last scene in *An Officer and a Gentleman*, where he grabs her up in his arms on the factory floor—" She let out a squeal as Jack swept her up, movie style. "What are you doing?"

"You want to be swept off your feet? I'm sweeping you off your feet."

She threw her arms around his neck with a smile that made his heart swell. But this wasn't a movie. He stopped and waited until he had her full attention.

"We still have a lot to talk about, Belle."

She chewed her lower lip. "I know. Clearly you have a lot to tell me about. And I've come to a few realizations myself."

He tipped his head back. "Oh, yeah? Like what?"

"Like I love you. Like I don't want us to be apart again. Oh, and I definitely want to discuss what you just said in the office." He managed to get the truck door open and slide her inside. She arched an eyebrow his way. "You know, that whole *woman I love* thing."

Jack stopped, standing beside the open door to the pickup in the parking lot of the office complex. Not exactly the romantic setting he'd hoped for, but he wasn't going to let her doubt his feelings for one more minute.

"You *are* the woman I love, Belle. You are the only woman I love, and the only woman I ever want to love." He looked down at the pavement for a moment before meeting her eyes. "I hurt you. And I'm sorry. I—"

"It's okay."

He pressed his lips together, shaking his head.

"It's not okay. Let me say this." She sat back and he continued, "I can't promise I'll never hurt you again, because we both know I can be stubborn and foolish. But I *can* promise that I'll try my damnedest not to hurt you again…ever. And I promise to—how did you say it?—fight for us when things get complicated. I will never give up on us again." He took her hand in his. "I need you too much."

Belle's eyes were shimmering with tears again. Jack was pretty sure they were the good kind, though. She lifted his hand to her lips and kissed his knuckles.

"I accept your apology. And I very much accept your love. And I accept your promise to work when things get tough." She lowered his hand back to her lap. "And I'm sorry for being so pushy. I'll work on that. Let's agree to be honest with each other, no matter what the issue is." He nodded, too overwhelmed with relief to speak. Then Belle winked at him. "And right now the issue is that it's about two hundred degrees inside this truck cab and I'm sweating right through this silk blouse. Get in here, turn on the air-conditioning and take me home."

Jack laughed and realized laughter didn't feel odd to him anymore. It felt right. Belle made him feel like smiling. And laughing. And loving. He tapped the brim of an imaginary hat to her.

"Your wish is my command, ma'am."

Chapter Seventeen

Belle handed Jack a beer and sat next to him on the cushioned glider with her wine in hand. The new glider on the veranda had been a surprise when they got home together. He told her he wanted a spot where they could sit and cuddle, instead of always sitting at the wooden picnic table. She definitely approved—of the comfort *and* the cuddling.

They sipped their drinks in silence, enjoying the soft, warm breeze and watching the sun settle low in the sky. It had been an emotionally exhausting day. Sarge, after nearly losing his mind with joy at Belle's arrival a few hours ago, was now curled at their feet, staring at Belle as if he was afraid she might vanish if he blinked.

Jack lifted his arm so she could scoot herself closer to his side. She knew he had to be even more wrung out than she was. Almost as soon as they'd sat down here, right after he'd swept her out of the office, things had turned serious.

He'd finally told her what happened overseas. The deadly attack. How it happened. Why he'd felt responsible. She thought of the men's faces she'd seen online—the three who'd died that day. She couldn't imagine the weight of taking on that kind of guilt. No wonder Jack had nightmares.

She'd listened in heartbroken silence as he talked about those men. And the ones who'd lived. Jack told her how he'd avoided his friend Steve's calls until Harper got on his case. That's when he'd told his sister about what happened, which seemed to have broken the dam of emotions he'd been struggling to contain. He said that, after Belle left him, he'd been inconsolable until his sister and Steve convinced him to go to counseling. Something he acknowledged that Belle had suggested a while ago. By the time he'd finished telling her about his first group session, Jack's body had been limp with exhaustion. Belle had made sandwiches for them, and now they watched the sunset together. They'd gotten through it. She took a sip of her wine, and felt Jack kissing the top of her head.

His voice was soft and low. "So now you know what a hot mess you've fallen in love with."

She turned to look up at him. "Bad stuff happened to you. You're dealing with it. That makes you the opposite of a hot mess." She smiled. "I have no regrets about falling in love with you."

"I don't know why you don't, but I'm glad."

"For lots of reasons. For one thing, you believe in me." Belle rested against him again, soaking up his warmth and calm strength. "I adore my family, but for a long time they acted like me opening my own boutique was some wildly impulsive move. I'm just the girl who loves to shop, so how could I be serious? You never once questioned my plan. You supported it and you had faith in my ability to do it, right from the start." Belle snuggled in closer, and Jack tightened his grip on her. "I'm glad you dared me to kiss you at the Valentine's Ball."

"Me, too, babe. Me, too."

Three nights later, they were in the same position on the veranda, once again watching the sunset. The new glider was quickly turning into one of Belle's favorite places. She'd made her grandmother's gumbo recipe for dinner, practicing her Louisiana cooking skills for next week's visit from her parents. Jack had offered the house as Mom and Dad's home base. It meant they were going to have a busy weekend painting and furnishing the guest room and spare bathroom, but she was looking forward to playing hostess.

Jack had seemed so much more settled since she'd moved back into the house. He'd barely begun his counseling journey, but he said he was already feeling relief from not having to bottle all that stress inside anymore. His first group session had shown him he wasn't alone. Now that he and Belle no longer had secrets hanging between them, he'd admitted that he was the happiest he ever remembered being in his life. She felt the same way. Life was better than good. It was wonderful.

Sarge seemed to be on the same page. Yesterday had been the first day the dog hadn't hidden his tennis ball in the closet. When Jack came in from the veranda that morning, he'd shown the ball to Belle in amazement.

"He left it for me to find, right near the steps to the yard. That's gotta be a good sign, right?"

She'd agreed, and they'd both heaped hugs and praise on Sarge. At the moment, he was sleeping near their feet. On his back. Three legs in the air. Snoring loudly.

Jack broke the silence with a chuckle. "That dog is definitely living his best life."

"I think all three of us are living our best lives, don't you?"

Before he could answer, his phone rang. Belle had to sit up to give him room to pull it out of his pocket. His eyebrows shot up in surprise before he answered it.

"Callum? What's up?"

Belle figured it was business talk, so she went inside to refill their drinks. When she came back out to the veranda, Jack was off the phone. He stared out over the backyard, so lost in thought that he jumped when she came over to the glider.

"Easy, tiger." Belle laughed, sitting next to him. She saw the blank look on his face and her laughter faded. "What's wrong? What did Callum want?"

He turned toward her, looking stunned. "He wants to give me money."

"Cool! He gave you a raise?"

"No." Jack shook his head. "Well, yes. I'm offi-cially off probation and I'll lead my own construc-tion crew on the next home build."

"Oh, Jack, I'm so happy for you. You deserve it." He still looked confused, though. She put her hand on his arm. "Okay, what has you so freaked out? What did he say?"

Jack blew out a long breath, his forehead fur-rowing. "Callum was talking to his sister, Steph-anie, at the veterinary clinic. I guess she told him about me placing Diva with Marcus, and how well Sarge was doing, and how I'd asked her to let me know about any hard-to-place animals that Paws and Claws rescue had."

Belle wasn't sure why he seemed so serious. "But that's a good thing, right? You want to place more animals with veterans who could use the companionship, and save the animals at the same time." They'd even come up with a name for it the other night—Pets2Vets. "Is Callum worried it will take your time away from the construction work? Because at this point it's barely an idea, so—"

"Callum wants to fund it."

Belle wasn't sure what to say. She'd offered to fund the charity idea originally, but Jack said he felt weird taking her money. He wanted her to use that for her boutique. Knowing Jack's concerns about the Fortune family's wealth, maybe Callum's offer had offended him?

He sat up before she could ask, shaking his head and finally smiling a little.

"Callum and his wife are setting up a charitable foundation under the Fortune Brothers Construction umbrella here in Rambling Rose. It's an idea the family came up with when they were building the Hotel Fortune and they got all that pushback from the locals." Belle nodded. She knew the story. "Callum's stepbrother, Wiley, suggested a charitable foundation might help make their community ties even stronger, and they're getting it started this year."

"But what does that have to do with Pets2Vets?"

"Callum said the foundation board wants to give me a grant to get it all started. They'll also help with the legal stuff, setting it up as a nonprofit and all that."

"Jack, that's amazing. But why do you seem so hesitant?"

"I don't know." He shrugged. "I guess it makes it real, and that's a little scary. What do I know about setting up a charity and getting something like this off the ground? What if I fail?"

"Oh, for heaven's sake." Belle grabbed his arm and lifted it so she could go under it and hug him. "It was your idea, and look how good at it you are already. Diva and Marcus are perfect together. And you said Marcus's neighbor lady was a vet who'd like a small dog and that Paws and Claws just rescued an older Pekinese who needs a quiet home. This thing is already 'off the ground' and you're doing great." She gave him a gentle pinch in the ribs. "And you're in love with the most organized woman in Rambling Rose, so you know I'll help you."

She raised her face in invitation, and he obliged her with a long, sweet kiss, tightening his arms around her. A thought crossed her mind and she began to giggle against his lips. Jack's eyes opened, filled with warmth and humor.

"I am afraid to ask what you're laughing about right now."

She gave him another quick kiss and sat up. "You know what Callum's call just did, don't you? His offer is *daring* you to follow your dream. Are you going to be brave enough to accept?"

Jack tipped his head back and laughed so long and so loud that Sarge flipped to his feet and looked at both of them in concern.

"Okay, you got me." Jack wiped his eyes, still chuckling. "Neither you nor I can say no to a dare. But I'll only accept this dare on one condition."

"What's that?"

"On second thought…two conditions." He took a sip of his beer, holding her tight against him with his other arm. "First, I'll need your help with this." She nodded, watching him set the beer glass on the nearby table.

"You know you have that."

"And second…" His expression grew more serious. "I'm giving *you* a dare, young lady."

"Oh, really? What is it?" She hoped it was a kiss—she'd really like to kiss him again. And again. All night long.

"Get going on your own dream, Belle. Follow

through on finding a location for Belle's Boutique. Make it happen."

Her heart was so full of love for this man who thought of her happiness in the midst of having his own dream come to life. She gave him a bright smile.

"I accept that dare. In fact, I've already been looking at locations. There's an older building near the center of town—an area that is being rehabilitated and becoming very trendy. But the building needs some love in order to really shine again." She stared deep into his coffee-colored eyes, seeing her own happy reflection there. "I'm thinking you might be just the guy to give it some love."

Jack stared back at her for a moment, and his mouth slid into a slow, sexy smile. He pulled her up onto his lap so effortlessly that she gave a squeak of surprise. Sarge looked between the two of them and apparently decided all was well. He plopped his head back down with a contented sigh. Jack cupped Belle's face in his hands.

"I'll try, but I'm not sure how much love I'll have to spare for a building after giving all my love to you. For the rest of my life, if you'll have me." His brows lowered for a second. "This isn't how I planned this moment, and I don't even have a ring yet, but—" Sarge chose that moment to let out a long, loud snore, and Jack laughed. "But I have a dog. And a house that's still too pink and way too big. And I have a job. And apparently I have a charity. And I have my heart, which you already own." He kissed her tenderly, and it felt full of promise. "So…what do you say, Belle? Are we taking the dare, for better or worse?" He pulled his head back, his voice raw with emotion. "Forever?"

She slid her arms around his neck. "That's not fair—you know I can't turn down a dare. I think I've loved you since you dared me at the Valentine's Ball." She leaned in for a kiss. "I'm yours, Jack Radcliffe. Forever."

* * * * *

*Look for the next book in the new
Harlequin Special Edition continuity
The Fortunes of Texas: The Wedding Gift*

Anyone but a Fortune

*by USA TODAY bestselling author
Judy Duarte*

*On sale March 2022 wherever Harlequin books
and ebooks are sold.*

*And catch up with the previous titles in
The Fortunes of Texas: The Wedding Gift:*

Their New Year's Beginning
by Michelle Major

*Available now, wherever Harlequin books
and ebooks are sold.*

WE HOPE YOU ENJOYED
THIS BOOK FROM

HARLEQUIN
SPECIAL
EDITION

Believe in love. Overcome obstacles. Find happiness.

Relate to finding comfort and strength in the
support of loved ones and enjoy the journey
no matter what life throws your way.

6 NEW BOOKS AVAILABLE EVERY MONTH!

COMING NEXT MONTH FROM

⒣ HARLEQUIN
SPECIAL EDITION

#2893 ANYONE BUT A FORTUNE
The Fortunes of Texas: The Wedding Gift • by Judy Duarte
Self-made woman Sofia De Leon has heard enough about the old-money Fortune family to know that Beau Fortune is not to be trusted. And now that they are competing for the same business award, he is also her direct rival. It is just a hot Texas minute, though, before ambition begins warring with attraction...

#2894 FIRST COMES BABY...
Wild Rose Sisters • by Christine Rimmer
When Josie LeClaire went into labor alone on her farm, she had no one to turn to but her nearby fellow farmer, Miles Halstead. Fortunately, the widowed Miles was more than up to the task. But a marriage of convenience is only convenient until one side ends up with unrequited feelings. Will Miles be willing to let go of his fears, or will Josie be the one left out in the cold?

#2895 HOME IS WHERE THE HOUND IS
Furever Yours • by Melissa Senate
Animal rescue worker Bethany Robeson already has her hands full with an inherited house and an overweight pooch named Meatball. She doesn't dare make room for Shane Dupree, her former high school sweetheart, now a single dad. Bethany doesn't believe in starting over, but Shane, baby Wyatt and Meatball could be the family she always dreamed of...

#2896 THE WRANGLER RIDES AGAIN
Men of the West • by Stella Bagwell
For years, rugged cowboy Jim Carroway has been more at home with horses than with people. But when stunning nanny Tallulah O'Brien arrives to wrangle the kids of Three Rivers Ranch, she soon tempts him from the barn back to life. After Jim lost his pregnant wife, he thought he'd closed his heart forever. Can the vibrant, vivacious Tally convince him that it's never too late for love's second act?

#2897 THE HERO NEXT DOOR
Small-Town Sweethearts • by Carrie Nichols
Olive Downing has big dreams for her Victorian bed-and-breakfast. She doesn't need her handsome new neighbor pointing out the flaws in her plan. But Cal Pope isn't the average busybody. The gruff firefighter can be sweet, charming—and the perfect partner for the town fundraiser. Maybe there's a soft heart underneath his rough exterior that needs rescuing, too?

#2898 A MARRIAGE OF BENEFITS
Home to Oak Hollow • by Makenna Lee
Veterinarian Jessica Talbot wants to build a clinic and wildlife rescue. She could access her trust fund, but there's a caveat—Jessica needs a husband. When she learns Officer Jake Carter needs funding to buy and train his own K-9 partner, Jessica proposes. Jake is shocked, but he agrees—only for the money. It's the perfect plan—if only Jessica can avoid falling for her husband...and vice versa!

YOU CAN FIND MORE INFORMATION ON UPCOMING HARLEQUIN TITLES, FREE EXCERPTS AND MORE AT HARLEQUIN.COM.

HSECNM0122B

"I remember. I remember it all, Bethany."

Jeez. He hadn't meant for his voice to turn so serious, so reverent. But there was very little chance of hiding his real feelings when she was around.

"Me, too," she said.

For a few moments they ate in silence.

"Thanks for helping me here," she said. "You've done a lot of that since I've been back."

"Anytime. And I mean that."

"Ditto," she said.

He reached over and squeezed her hand but didn't let go. And suddenly he was looking—with that seriousness, with that reverence—into those green eyes that had also kept him up those nights when he couldn't stop thinking about her. They both leaned in at the same time, the kiss soft, tender, then with all the pent-up passion they'd clearly both been feeling these last days.

She pulled slightly away. "Uh-oh."

He let out a rough exhale, trying to pull himself together. "Right? You're leaving in a couple weeks. Maybe three tops. And I'm solely focused on being the best father I can be. So that's two really good reasons why we shouldn't kiss again." Except he leaned in again.

And so did she. This time there was nothing soft or tender about the kiss. Instead, it was pure passion. His hand wound in her silky brown hair, her hands on his face.

A puppy started barking, then another, then yet another. The three cockapoos.

"They're saving us from getting into trouble," Bethany said, glancing at the time on her phone. "Time for their potty break. They'll be interrupting us all night, so that should keep us in line."

He smiled. "We can get into a lot of trouble in between, though."

Don't miss
Home is Where the Hound Is *by Melissa Senate,*
available March 2022 wherever
Harlequin Special Edition books and ebooks are sold.

Harlequin.com